Testaments

Ohio University Press Polish and Polish-American Studies Series

Series Editor: John J. Bukowczyk

Framing the Polish Home: Postwar Cultural Constructions of Hearth, Nation, and Self, edited by Bożena Shallcross

Traitors and True Poles: Narrating a Polish-American Identity, 1880–1939, by Karen Majewski

Auschwitz, Poland, and the Politics of Commemoration, 1945–1979, by Jonathan Huener

The Exile Mission: The Polish Political Diaspora and Polish Americans, 1939–1956, by Anna D. Jaroszyńska-Kirchmann

The Grasinski Girls: The Choices They Had and the Choices They Made, by Mary Patrice Erdmans

Testaments: Two Novellas of Emigration and Exile, by Danuta Mostwin

Testaments

Two Novellas of
Emigration and Exile

Danuta Mostwin

Translated from the original Polish by
Marta Erdman and Nina Dyke

OHIO UNIVERSITY PRESS

ATHENS

Ohio University Press, Athens, Ohio 45701
© 2005 by Ohio University Press
www.ohiou.edu/oupress
Printed in the United States of America
All rights reserved

Ohio University Press books are printed on acid-free paper ∞

13 12 11 10 09 08 07 06 05   5 4 3 2 1
Cover photo by Jacek Lech Mostwin

Library of Congress Cataloging-in-Publication Data

Mostwin, Danuta.
  [Testament Blazeja. English]
  Testaments : two novellas of emigration and exile / Danuta Mostwin ;
translated from the original Polish by Marta Erdman and Nina Dyke.— 1st ed.
      p. cm. — (Ohio University Press Polish and Polish-American studies
series)   Includes bibliographical references.
   ISBN 0-8214-1607-3 (cloth : alk. paper) — ISBN 0-8214-1608-1 (pbk. :
alk. paper)   1. Mostwin, Danuta—Translations into English.   I. Erdman,
Marta, 1921–1982. II. Dyke, Nina. III. Mostwin, Danuta. Jokasta. English.
IV. Title. V. Series.   PG7158.M64T4713 2005
   891.8'5373—dc22
                                           2005002787

Publication of books in the Polish and Polish-American Studies Series has been made possible in part by the generous support of the following organizations:

Polish American Historical Association, New Britain, Connecticut

Stanislaus A. Blejwas Endowed Chair in Polish and Polish American Studies, Central Connecticut State University, New Britain, Connecticut

The Polish Institute of Arts and Sciences of America, Inc., New York, New York

The Piast Institute: An Institute for Polish and Polish American Affairs, Detroit, Michigan

Contents

Series Editor's Preface

THE IMMIGRANT AGED, "the last of the first" as they have been called, experienced remarkable changes and transformations, both societal and personal, as they left or were expelled from the lands of their birth and started new lives for themselves abroad in places like America. Walls of language and privacy often stood between them and their grandchildren, barring them from telling their often poignant stories until death silenced their lips forever. But these elderly immigrants lived lives of hope and hurt, joy and sorrow, aspiration and resignation, lives worth remembering and recording. In *Testaments: Two Novellas of Emigration and Exile,* Danuta Mostwin recovers two such bittersweet stories of yesterday's disappointments and tomorrow's dreams.

Herself a World War II–era émigré, Danuta Mostwin is both an accomplished scholar and a well-published novelist whose fiction hitherto has remained untranslated, known almost exclusively to Polish-language readers in the United States and in her native Poland. The English translations of the two novellas presented here, *Jocasta* and *The Last Will of Blaise Twardowski,* represent the first complete works made accessible to the English-speaking public. Those who venture within the covers of this slim volume will be both touched and taught. Readers never again will see the old immigrant man or the elderly émigré woman the same way they may have seen them—or just looked past them—before encountering the memorable characters in Danuta Mostwin's two stories. Scholars, students, and general readers will find themselves changed by this book.

Testaments: Two Novellas of Emigration and Exile is the sixth volume in the Ohio University Press Polish and Polish-American Studies Series. The series revisits the historical and contemporary experience of one of America's largest European ethnic groups and the history of a European homeland that has played a disproportionately important role in twentieth-century and contemporary world affairs. The series aims to publish innovative monographs and more general works that investigate under- or unexplored topics or themes that offer new, critical, revisionist, or comparative perspectives in the area of Polish and Polish-American studies. Interdisciplinary or multidisciplinary in profile, the series seeks manuscripts on Polish immigration and ethnic communities, the country of origin, and its various peoples in history, anthropology, cultural studies, political economy, current politics, and related fields.

Publication of the Ohio University Press Polish and Polish-American Studies Series marks a milestone in the maturation of the Polish studies field and stands as a fitting tribute to the scholars and organizations whose efforts have brought it to fruition. Supported by a series advisory board of accomplished Polonists and Polish-Americanists, the Polish and Polish-American Studies Series has been made possible through generous financial assistance from the Polish American Historical Association, the Polish Institute of Arts and Sciences of America, the Stanislaus A. Blejwas Endowed Chair in Polish and Polish American Studies at Central Connecticut State University, Madonna University, and the Piast Institute and through institutional support from Wayne State University and Ohio University Press. Among the individuals who have helped bring this work into print, our special thanks go to Professor John Kromkowski of the Catholic University of America in Washington, D.C., who, unsolicited, first brought the translations of Danuta Mostwin's work to our attention, and to Professor Joanna Rostropowicz Clark and Professor Thomas J. Napierkowski, who lent the project their expertise by writing, respectively, an introduction and an afterword for the book. The series meanwhile has benefited from the warm encouragement of a number of other persons, including Gillian Berchowitz, M. B. B. Biskupski, the late Stanislaus A. Blejwas, Mary Erdmans, Thaddeus Gromada, Sister Rose Marie Kujawa, CSSF, James S. Pula, Thaddeus Radzilowski, and David Sanders. The moral and material support from all of these institutions and individuals is gratefully acknowledged.

John J. Bukowczyk

Guide to Pronunciation

THE FOLLOWING KEY provides a guide to the pronunciation of Polish words and names.

a is pronounced as in *father*

c as ts in *cats*

ch like a guttural h

cz as hard ch in *church*

g always hard, as in *get*

i as ee

j as y in *yellow*

rz like French j in *jardin*

sz as sh in *ship*

szcz as shch, enunciating both sounds, as in *fresh cheese*

u as oo in *boot*

w as v

ć as soft ch

ś as sh

ż, ź both as zh, the latter higher in pitch than the former

ó as oo in boot

ą as French *on*

ę as French *en*

ł as w

ń changes the combinations -in to -ine, -en to -ene, and -on to -oyne

The accent in Polish words always falls on the penultimate syllable.

Danuta Mostwin's Puzzles of Identity

"EXILE IS IN FASHION," writes Ian Buruma, himself an exile from several countries and cultures, in his essay "The Romance of Exile." "Today," he goes on to quote the Polish-Jewish writer Eva Hoffman, "'at least within the framework of postmodern theory, we have come to value exactly those qualities of experience that exile demands—uncertainty, displacement, the fragmented identity. Within this conceptual framework, exile becomes, well, sexy, glamorous, interesting.'"[1] And, of course, an exile is an ultimate *other*, but in ways more complex and, for the majority of exiles and emigrants, far less glamorous than their image in postmodern theories.

To begin with, few exiles today are called by this romantic name. They are much more likely to fall into the crowded category of "refugees" and soon thereafter to merge into the even less significant mass of "immigrants." Even now, despite enormous progress in the Western democracies toward cultural open-mindedness, some exiles are more acceptable—and more fashionable—than others. After World War II, refugees from Poland came to the United States with at least somewhat justified expectations of an appreciative welcome, if only because they had fought the Nazis for the longest period of time and on all fronts. If not glamorous, they were certainly—most of them—heroic. Yet they came to a world whose knowledge of what they had done and experienced was very limited. The Americans knew next to nothing about the near extermination of European Jewish communities (the term "Holocaust" did not appear until the late 1950s), and they had but a vague notion of the horrors that had been inflicted on Poland by both her totalitarian neighbors, Nazi Germany and the communist Soviet Union. Few had heard about the Warsaw Ghetto Uprising in 1943 or the Warsaw Uprising in 1944, and practically no information existed in the West about Soviet wartime crimes against non-Russian populations in the occupied territories stretching from the Baltic to the Black Sea. When such information did emerge—as in the case of the Katyń Forest Massacre, in which fourteen thousand Polish military officers were executed—it was vigorously suppressed for reasons of realpolitik and pro-Russian sentiment: the Soviet Union was then, if only for a short time, a deservedly celebrated ally.

In his speech accepting the 1980 Nobel Prize for Literature, Czesław Miłosz said that "those who come from the 'other Europe,' wherever they find themselves, notice to what extent their experience isolates them from their new milieu—and this may become the source of a new obsession." The effects of this isolation on the majority of post–World War II Polish (and not only Polish) émigré writers were quite predictable: severe depression, suicide, and a creative output limited to themes of recent national traumas, which, one should add, could not be explored freely in Soviet-controlled postwar Poland. Gradually, though, some of the younger or emotionally stronger writers and poets began to involve their art with the immediate reality of the immigrant condition and, therefore, with the reality of America. The most remarkable voice in this small group belongs to Danuta Mostwin, a former Warsaw medical student who began her writing career in this country in the city of Baltimore—away from the Polish émigré enclaves of New York and Washington and, therefore, away from any semblance of exile's glamour.

Born in 1921 in Lublin, Danuta Mostwin came of age in wartime Warsaw, where, after graduating from the prestigious Emilia Plater Gymnasium, she enrolled in the clandestine medical academy.[2] Her father, a professional military officer, fought in the 1939 campaign and during the remaining years of World War II participated in Allied war efforts on the western front. Danuta's mother, from her Warsaw apartment in the Saska Kępa district, joined the Armia Krajowa (Home Army) network of underground resistance operations. Her address became a haven for military emissaries of the Polish government in exile. One of them, a young captain named Stanisław Bask-Mostwin, parachuted into Poland in the spring of 1944 to deliver two hundred thousand dollars to Żegota,[3] but stayed on and married Danuta. After the war, fearing arrest by the new communist authorities, the couple and Danuta's mother illegally crossed the border into Czechoslovakia and then trekked to Western Europe, where they were reunited with Danuta's father.

They had intended to settle in London but, like hundreds of other demo-bilized Polish soldiers, they felt stranded in England, where, after an abrupt transition from military to civilian status, they were regarded with a mixture of guilt and xenophobia. Their military pensions running out, they were left to their own pitiable devices. In 1951 the entire family, which by then included the young couple's son, left for the United States. Although they no longer expected a hero's welcome, they were not prepared for the air of general in-difference manifested, above all, in a total lack of assistance in their efforts to find employment. As foreigners, the two former officers could not benefit from the G.I. Bill, and Danuta's medical training in Poland, without proper certificates or local connections, appeared to be worthless. Coming from a military rather than an intellectual background, they did not belong to the small, struggling, but mutually supportive Polish cultural elite in New York. Instead, they found themselves among a much larger crowd of Poles and Pol-ish Jews in circumstances similar to their own. Finally, unable to find jobs in the New York metropolitan area, they boarded a train to Baltimore. There, homeless and penniless, they turned for help to the local Polish-American community, descendants of Polish peasant immigrants from a previous era. Thus began their life in the New World, at the bottom of its socioeconomic ladder.

In those circumstances, Danuta Mostwin, now the wife of a factory worker and mother of a small child, gave up all hope of becoming a medical doctor. She did, however, take college courses in social work, graduating with honors, and eventually received a PhD in social science from Columbia University. She also began to write fiction. In 1958 her first novel, *Dom starej lady* (House of the Old Lady), was published in London by Katolicki Ośrodek Wydawniczy "Veritas." It was an autobiographical account of the harrowing, humiliating experiences of Polish refugees in postwar London. Yet Mostwin perceived an element of comedy in the situation, the classic motif of the reversal of fortune. The male characters in the novel are former war heroes—men who flew RAF planes in the Battle of Britain and fought at Monte Cassino, in North Africa, and in the Warsaw Uprising—who are learning how to become bakers, plumbers, and upholsterers. The female characters are more resilient, but they too tire of exploring ever-diminishing and more elusive prospects for escaping the London slums. Mostwin nar-rates the story from the perspective of a participating observer, in a voice that accommodates both irony and compassion, a style that would become her artistic trademark.

Rare in Poland's postwar fiction, this slightly detached relationship between the narrator and the other characters is also typical of Henryk Grynberg's documentary novels about the few survivors of his Jewish community in Poland. Like Mostwin's displaced and degraded war heroes in *Dom starej lady*, Grynberg's victims appear even more tragic because of the comical aspects of their inept efforts to cope with the catastrophe, the total destruction, of their former existence. These two very different writers share another trait characteristically absent from mainstream Polish fiction in the second half of the twentieth century: their attention to the importance of family histories and emotional connections. Wartime death (for Grynberg, the death of his father and his younger brother; for Mostwin the murder of her beloved uncle and his daughter by the Gestapo) and separations resulting from deportation and exile deepened their appreciation of family bonds and the value of loss followed by return. Because the real Polish family rarely had a history that fit the prescribed norms of ideological correctness, writers in postwar Poland tended to create characters whose family backgrounds were vague or unknown: tormented, lonely runaways from their own pasts. The task of rescuing the Polish twentieth-century family from literary oblivion thus was left to the émigré writers. Some—most notably Maria Kuncewicz, Czesław Miłosz, Józef Mackiewicz, and Danuta Mostwin—met the challenge, while others, lacking the psychological and financial resources to complete larger projects, failed. It is, perhaps, not surprising that Danuta Mostwin, trained in medicine and social psychology, would insist that, in order to effectively function in their adoptive country, immigrants had to harmonize their connection to ancestral culture with a willingness to adapt to the way of life of a local society: to become at home away from home.

In her doctoral dissertation—based on numerous interviews and case studies—Mostwin developed the concept of "a third value" as a selective merger of the old and the new ways of life. She wrote: "The process of the emergence of this third value within an uprooted immigrant's personality may thus be described as the creation of a new form of cultural identity that is neither with the country of origin nor with the receiving country, but constitutes a third value, the integration of selective cultural patterns specific for the individual and for his unique situation of uprootment."[4]

That this process is often resisted by its participants and hampered by multiple external obstacles interested Danuta Mostwin, both as a writer and as a social scientist, no less than did finding prescriptions for its success. In her next two novels—the lighthearted *Ameryko! Ameryko!* (America! America!), published in 1961 by Polska Fundacja Kulturalna in London, and the much darker *Ja za wodą, ty za wodą* (Beyond the Waters, You and I), published in 1972 by Instytut Literacki in Paris—some of the characters rationalize their resistance to acculturation by way of social prejudices or generalized political resentments. They might be jarred by specific local customs or by the incomprehensible bureaucracy of American institutions, or they might invoke the ever-festering wound of Poland's betrayal at Yalta. Again, the apparent loss of a former identity and with it the basis for high self-esteem, causes profound emotional pain, particularly in the older male members of the small circle of recent emigrants.

In *Ameryko! Ameryko!*, it is Colonel Józef Żuławski—the character modeled on the author's father—who explodes into uncontrollable rage whenever teenage customers of the cheap cafeteria that he owns call him "Joe." He is, of course, simply irritated by the American brats' disrespect for an older man, the kind of behavior that would not have been tolerated in Poland. But beyond this cultural clash, on a deeper level, he experiences a frightful confusion about his present identity. As a military officer he had seen himself as he was regarded by others, according to his rank and uniform; now, aproned, dishrag in hand, he indeed might have become this new, arrogant world's Joe, while knowledge of his true person has shrunk to the tiny circle of his immediate family. Mostwin approaches Żuławski's crisis of identity with a wonderful, self-deprecating (he is, after all, *her* father figure) sense of humor, not unlike that of many so-called ethnic comedians in America: Irish, Jewish, and African American. She pokes fun at stereotypes on both sides of the cultural dividing lines. We laugh at the absurdity of Żuławski's fury, yet, at the same time, we relate to his pain and humiliation because we all, the immigrant readers of her novel, had to endure similar struggles: to sell ourselves cheap, to have our identities—even our names—cut short. In *Ameryko! Ameryko!* Mostwin's fictional immigrant family is cured of prejudice when their new house, in the American-American neighborhood, burns down, and dozens of the hitherto unknown neighbors rush to help.

Ja za wodą, ty za wodą tells the story of an encounter between the immigrant Polish community and two visitors from the People's Republic of Poland, who come to Baltimore on research grants from the U.S. government during a brief thaw in the Cold War, after 1956. Mostwin employs here another classic comic device: the disruption of stability by the arrival of a stranger. But the comedy in this meeting of two worlds—oddly close and oddly distant—is much darker and more complex than that in Mostwin's previous two novels; its tensions remain unresolved, and the ending lacks the upbeat promise of "the third value." Set, like *Ameryko! Ameryko!,* in a fictionalized Baltimore, the novel's cast of characters does not include anyone resembling members of the author's family, a circumstance that frees her from the inhibitions inherent in using autobiographical material. We meet a familiar group of recent immigrants who, a decade into their lives in the United States, have somewhat reluctantly integrated with the old Polonia but remain unconnected to American society at large. They cling to symbols of patriotism but shield themselves from the reality of Poland, and their resolve to return there at some politically favorable point in the future is clearly diminished. Caught in such a web of identity anxiety, they are half-disapproving and half-proud of one member of the group, Hanka Sanocka, a successful medical doctor who has come to terms with the cultural transition and is determined to make the best of her new American citizenship, both for herself and for her two daughters. Her wholehearted acceptance of the American way of life is not shared by her husband, who still clings to patriotic ideals and would like to take his family back to Poland, communist or not. Their marital discord comes forth when Hanka finds herself attracted to Doctor Kettler, one of two Polish beneficiaries of a grant for a one-year residence at Johns Hopkins. The attraction is as mutual as it is unsettling for both of these unsentimental careerists. A car accident, in which Hanka is critically injured on the way to their first date, prevents the development of the affair and solves Kettler's dilemma: to stay, or to return. A similar dilemma is experienced by the other doctor-scholar from Poland, a shy, married woman named Joasia, who becomes involved romantically with an American colleague at the Johns Hopkins Hospital. But she, too, decides to return to her husband and son in Warsaw, leaving behind her American admirer.

Although some reviewers in prestigious émigré literary magazines recognized the overall artistic strength of the novel and welcomed Mostwin as a truly original voice from the Polish diaspora in America, others balked at her depressing portrait of the immigrant ghetto, underscored by the decision of the two visitors to go back to their blighted homeland, rather than to "choose freedom." Mostwin's honesty and her realist talent might have brought her a more resounding success with the truth-starved readers in Poland, but again this chance could not but be lost. The reception of both novels by émigré critics was muted. They praised Mostwin's talent of observation and her realism, but seemed uncomfortable with her unorthodox approach to dealing with the tragedy of Poland and with the cruel fate of Polish war heroes. *Ameryko! Ameryko!* was published in Poland in 1981, in a tiny edition, and with little notice at the time of yet another national trauma—the brutal suppression of the Solidarity movement. *Ja za wodą, ty za wodą* had to wait until the fall of communism in Poland.

A different confrontation between two worlds occurs in Mostwin's non-immigrant (so to speak) novel, *Olivia,* published by Instytut Kulturalny in Paris in 1965. One world is represented by a Polish-American therapist, who narrates the story—the other, by her patient, or "case," a troubled young American woman named Olivia. Olivia is a runaway from her adoptive, un-loving, and unloved, parents. She has a severe drug problem and, conse-quently, is incapable of maintaining any relationship, including the one with her therapist. There is a masterfully explored parallel between the successful "adoption" of the therapist into her new country and the failed adoption of Olivia into her new family, a failure that sets the young protagonist on a course of self-destruction. The therapist's efforts to unravel the tangle of external and internal causes of Olivia's misery bring no answers; at the end she loses the case. Olivia, true to the mysterious nature of her malady, disappears. That fail-ure forces the therapist to turn the mirror on herself: was she unable to make the meaningful contact with Olivia because of or in spite of her own "other-ness"? Did Olivia "punish" her as yet another substitute parental figure, or did she, the overcurious therapist, invite the punishment by straying from strictly professional interest in the case? We can also interpret *Olivia* as a record of the turning point in one immigrant's journey from the "outside" to the "inside" of her adoptive/adopted country. For now, not only is she entitled to deal with the suffering of a native-born American, but she can afford either to pass or to fail the test. In writing *Olivia,* Mostwin graduated from one school of pain, that of her fellow exiles, to the all-inclusive class of universal ills.

Mostwin continued both to counsel and to write. Her caseload, mostly elderly and poor inhabitants of Baltimore's immigrant district, grew into a portfolio of short stories, and the collection *Asteroidy* (Asteroids) came out in 1968 from Polska Fundacja Kulturalna in London. Dignified in their suffering, accepting of lifelong hardship as uneducated laborers, these men and women of distant Slavic roots had a different effect on Mostwin's craft than had her own milieu of postwar refugees. Absent are her tendency toward satire, her often bitter irony, and the intricate play of multimirrored reflections of the observer and the observed. The *Asteroids* stories, like their protagonists, are stark and deceptively simple. While the American social worker in Mostwin filed her case paperwork in English, the Polish writer peered beyond the routine questions and hesitant answers into the scarcely articulable, but always distinct, mystery of human fate—a mystery all the more compelling for the poverty of the subjects' vocabulary of self-knowledge.

In the first of the two novellas selected for this volume, Błażej Twardowski is an old, ailing immigrant, a Polish peasant who came to America as a teenage boy. He never married and now, knowing that his end is near, he wonders to whom should he will his life's savings. He never spent any money on himself, so the sum is not negligible—but he has no immediate relatives. There is a distant cousin in Pennsylvania, whom he meets, and the families of his sister and his stepbrother in Poland, none of whose many members he had ever seen. He asks a local Polish travel agent for help, and this not unkind intermediary writes and translates letters between the contending parties. The letters from Poland are, of course, outrageously solicitous and full of invented woes and make-believe disasters. Although the translator alerts Błażej to these deceptions, the old man is transfixed by the language of the letters, by their flamboyant phraseology and descriptions of farm life—a life that seems all the more enticing, the nearer its presumed extinction without an instant infusion of cash from "Beloved Uncle." Błażej is not fooled—but he pretends that he is and sends the cash. What he really pays for is not a new barn, a replaced roof, and cures for every sick pig or child, but the flowery, greed-inspired prose of these letters and the childhood memories they evoke. Besides, he understands greed and thrift, and he doesn't really mind contributing to the enrichment of those who are, after all, his kinfolk. The cousin from Pennsylvania, on the other hand—although equally greedy—can no longer produce a properly embellished Polish sentence, and she also fails to visit him more than once in the hospital during his final illness. Alone all his life, the laborer Błażej will, however, have a true friend at his deathbed: an educated man, the Polish translator.

The second novella, *Jocasta,* explores a more pathological landscape of the human soul in a mutually destructive relationship between mother and son. The mother's love is sick: it ruins the son's marriage and literally drives him insane. But as in *Olivia,* the reader never gets to the bottom of what caused the misery: war, separation after the son's emigration, and the mother's long stay in Warsaw until she could come to the United States? Or was it all triggered by the son's marriage to a German woman? The story represents Mostwin's deepening interest in the corrosive effects of conflicts of identity, in ways that are as incomprehensible to participants in the drama as they are to outside observers.

Before returning in her most recent fiction to the theme of the fragmented and increasingly bleak—few of the old soldiers age well, and many die—émigré experience, Mostwin completed a cycle of four novels that tells the story of one extended family, based on her own, in a time frame that stretches from World War I to the aftermath of World War II. The notion to begin the project came to Mostwin during a visit to Poland in 1961, her first since she had left the country in 1945. This reunion with relatives of her parents' generation and the powerful jolt of memories provided instant inspiration, but the stamina that the project required came, as she would often remark, from her American education in perseverance. In one of her articles on the benefits of emigration, she wrote about the American ideals and values that she tried to incorporate in her work as a Polish writer: "First, the value of the individual. Of the uniqueness and irreplaceability of every human being. The value that surpasses a group or a society. Second, the idea of creative change. Opportunity for self-enrichment with that which is new and contemporary but which doesn't shun the past, or what is sometimes called 'the burden of history.' In my work, both that of the writer and that of the scholar, I have pointed to the ways of achieving such fullness."[5]

In her "Polish" novels, Mostwin addressed the burden of history. There are countries, Poland and Russia among them, where literature is the primary source of knowledge about history because novels are not as easily censored as school textbooks. Historical figures appear only in the background, while the main narrative belongs to a cluster of fictional families, actors in and victims of historic events. Mostwin chose her own family, socially mobile and politically active, and began its story as far back as oral testimonies and preserved documents could pass it on to her. The first and the second books in the cycle, *Cień księdza Piotra* (The Shadow of Father Piotr) and *Szmaragdowa zjawa* (The Emerald Specter), take the reader back to the time of the re-emergence of independent Poland during and after World War I. Political matters in these novels—and no personal space there is untouched by intrusion of politics—could not be discussed openly in the People's Republic of Poland. Mostwin knew it, of course, and did her expert best to enter the forbidden zones.

But it is the third novel of the cycle, *Tajemnica zwyciężonych* (The Secret of the Vanquished), published in London in 1992, that most conspicuously enters uncharted territory: the Polish family in World War II. The outbreak of the war coincided with Mostwin's coming of age: she had turned eighteen in 1939 and therefore could rely here on her own memories, conversations with relatives, the recollections of her husband (who provided her with detailed descriptions of several World War II battles), and a variety of preserved documents. The military history parallels that of Mostwin's extended family: the German occupation of Warsaw and Lublin, the underground activities of practically every relative and friend, the Jewish ghetto in Lublin, heroes, martyrs, traitors. What distinguishes the novel from most other fictionalized accounts of the period in Polish literature is its bracing disregard for political and artistic trends—the latter often serving as strategies to circumvent the former. One may say that here Mostwin rolled up her sleeves and stepped into a locked-up house to recover its unclaimed contents. And this time she went after truth that had been kept secret not because of personal denials and self-deceptions but because of a grand denial by a punitive political system. The denial—which at first had been total, but then gradually weakened and allowed trickles of veracity—concerned all Polish World War II military efforts other than those approved by the Kremlin; the Molotov-Ribbentrop Pact to collaborate in the destruction of Poland; the Soviet policy of standing idly by during the 1944 Warsaw Uprising; the persecution of military personnel and of vast categories of the civilian population of the territories annexed by the Soviet Union in 1939 and under the communist regime in "liberated" Poland. There were also some secrets and distortions of truth on the Western side of the postwar political landscape which, in most general terms, related to the betrayal of Poland by the Allies. Where choice was possible, however, between the bitter and the poisoned cup, Polish freedom fighters opted for emigration to Western Europe, Israel, and the Americas. The escape of the three main protagonists in *Tajemnica* is the subject of the short final volume of Mostwin's family saga, *Nie ma domu* (There Is No Home), published in Poland in 1996.

Home and house, dwellings that need to be fixed or that are beyond repair, austere rented rooms, flower-filled villas, and dreary hospital rooms—these are Mostwin's signature *topoi,* and they owe their function and appearance both to the individual traits of their inhabitants and to verdicts of history. The home-centeredness of Mostwin's imagination may be attributed to her being a woman writer, perhaps in the same way that her interest in fractured identities is a mark of an émigré writer. When one reviewer praised the "masculine maturity" of her later novels, Mostwin promptly identified his remark as symptomatic of male chauvinism, Polish style. It is true that her female characters are seldom weak or meek and that they may be more adaptable to traumatic reversals of fortune than their male companions. Yet men and women in Mostwin's fiction are equally capable of great courage and integrity in the face of mortal threat and they are equally, if differently, susceptible to the pain of permanent displacement.

One area in which Mostwin's gender has mattered is that of the reception of her work in Poland. When her novels *The Shadow of Father Piotr* and *The Emerald Specter* were published in Poland in 1985 and 1988—both in very small editions—her name was familiar to only a handful of well-informed readers, and, partly because the entire country was deeply preoccupied with the current political situation (the crushing of the Solidarity movement), the books received scant notice. But male émigré writers, whose works were then beginning to be published or circulated in smuggled copies—some of long-established fame, like Witold Gombrowicz and Czesław Miłosz, others younger and less known—fared much better, preceded by an esteem that traditionally glorified the male exile artist, the émigré poet who, in an old Polish expression, had fought with the pen for the fatherland's freedom. For forty (yes!) years, Danuta Mostwin had done just that at her home-away-from-home in Baltimore. But in addition to patriotic lore, her typewriter also produced works of broader significance—studies in the contemporary condition of uprootment that are universal and do not require explanatory notes about

Polish history. As she examined the fates of the protagonists of her stories, as she transformed living men, women, and children into fictional characters, she continued to discover that external forces in human experience—exile, war, poverty, participation in collective catastrophes or victories—account for only some answers about the trajectory of a life and may reveal as often as conceal the essence of individual existence. In getting close to the point of fusion of the historical and the personal elements of identity, Mostwin attained her very own artistic "third value."

Danuta Mostwin's collected works are at last coming out in Poland, issued by Oficyna Wydawnicza Kucharski in Toruń. That this event coincides with the publication of the present book, the first rendering of her fiction into English, signifies a belated turning point in this outstanding writer's voyage between the old and the new worlds and in time zones that she continues to expand.

Joanna Rostropowicz Clark

Notes

1. Ian Buruma, "The Romance of Exile: Real Wounds, Unreal Wounds," *New Republic,* February 12, 2001, 33.

2. Under German occupation, Poles were not allowed to attend secondary or college-level schools.

3. An underground organization that assisted Polish Jews.

4. Danuta Mostwin, "Uprootment and Anxiety," *International Journal of Mental Health* 5, no. 2 (1976): 113.

5. Danuta Mostwin, "Podróż w dwóch czasach: O emigracji i literaturze emigracyjnej" [A Voyage in Two Time Zones: On Emigration and Émigré Literature] in *Słyszę jak śpiewa Ameryka* [I Hear America Singing] (London: Polska Fundacja Kulturalna, 1998), 271.

The Last Will of Blaise Twardowski

Now that Błażej is no longer here, his last will can be opened. But which one? For there are two of them. Which one is more important? Which one will be upheld in court—for that's the way things are heading, no doubt about that. Two wills. Two pages in an atlas. Two halves of the globe. And between them, Błażej Twardowski. That's what it has come to, finally, that's how important he got to be. Although out of this life himself, he still straddles the line dividing two worlds.

A sunken face in the sheltering shadow of an oxygen tent, cheeks made gaunt by the removal of his dentures: that's Błażej. And that's his hand stretched out from under the plastic curtain, groping haltingly on top of the hospital blanket.

Błażej cackles.

"Vooltures, vooltures . . . scum . . . they're no good . . . all of them just waiting, just waiting, just waiting . . . vooltures . . . ."

Błażej implores.

"Promise me . . . swear you'll do it . . . my last will . . . ."

Błażej beseeches with his outstretched hand, with the waning whisper of his once mighty voice.

"My last will . . . ."

|||

Perhaps one should take a good look at Błażej himself, for, although he became a personage in his own right, a man to reckon with, because of these two wills, he was there all along for nearly eighty years. Błażej belonged to Broad Street. Is there anyone who does not know Broad Street? It runs from the bay all the way to the hospital and ends beyond. Although it is the part closer to the bay, uncared for and pockmarked in spots, that was truly Błażej's street, one cannot avoid looking at the hospital, a huge labyrinthine snail with a green dome and additions stuck on here and there.

When Błażej walked along Broad Street, it seemed as though he had come into the world right there and would also meet his end there. Many people thought so. The organist, for one. He says: "That one from Broad Street. You know who I mean . . . Twardowski." He doesn't even remember Błażej's name nor does he think that anything in Błażej's life could ever have happened away from Broad Street. And yet he had collected a commission and made some money because of the old man. The same with the lawyer. To him, Błażej was just another case. Only Wieniawski knew perhaps a little more about Błażej and, having won the old man's trust, he had acquired a burden he had to carry until the very end.

There were two other things in Błażej's life besides Broad Street: his native village and the steel mill. His village was in the old country—an ordinary, poverty-stricken village amid sprawling flat fields, with a church and a graveyard. The village didn't even have any orchards, just an apple tree or a pear tree in back of some of the houses. Tillable land was what counted. Everyone there was greedy for land.

Błażej remembered some songs from his village days. A beer or two at the Polish Home bar would bring them all back to him, especially this one:

> There goes that girl from Lepowiec,
> Her rump wiggling like a ewe,
> "What have you got there, pretty maid,
> "What have you got under your apron?"
> "Do not ask me what I have got,
> "Come this evening, I will show you."
> Evening came, but she did not,
> She just laughed at him.

But that wasn't the most important thing. What was important was that in that village he had learned first to spell and later to read and write. There had been a boy there, not much older than Błażej, who had been sent to the city, to schools, to study for the priesthood. Błażej had become good friends with that Jasiek Lipa. To tell the truth, it was Jasiek who chose Błażej as a friend, and Błażej who surrendered slowly and cautiously at first, then totally, with all his heart, even though he did not realize at the time the strength of this friendship. Had Jasiek not come forth first, had he not taken the first step, Błażej never would have dared. More likely, he would have stood to the side jeering. But the other one came first and said: " I'll teach you, Błażek." Mother had fussed that no one had that kind of money to pay for lessons. But the other one cared nothing for money. He was full of the things they had stuffed into his head. He wanted to talk, to share, and he chose Błażej. Was it because Błażej was taller and stronger than other boys, or was it because he was an orphan and his stepfather was quick with the belt? No one knows. Mistrustful, but proud to be chosen, Błażej went to Jasiek, and they became like a pair of scales unequally weighted. Strangely, something made them balance one another to perfection. Jasiek would say, "Just you wait, Błażek. Come fall, you'll be able to read and you'll write me a letter, too." And Błażej would reply, "Some day I'll pay you back. I'll thank you some day." He did not know that he was already repaying and thanking Jasiek by giving him his trust.

Jasiek returned to the seminary, and Błażek left the village. Other, more important events rushed by. Youth burned out quickly, and Błażej saw no sense in poking in the ashes. He forgot about Jasiek and about the village and its affairs, too. He was no longer "Błażek" but "Mister Blaise Twardowski." There was no room in his new life for the village or Jasiek Lipa—or even a memory of them—or any remembrance of that gratitude of long ago or of that feeling of trust, once coaxed into life and now buried forever in the ashes of an abandoned fire.

"What did anyone ever give me there?" Błażej would say. "An empty belly, that's what. There was nothing to eat there. You couldn't buy a pair of shoes."

There was only Błażej Twardowski, the steelworks, and Broad Street. Broad Street, the line of Life on the open palm of the city. It begins near the bay, where Błażej had landed. First it runs straight and even, then it rises, climbs higher and higher, passes by the Polish Home and its restaurant, past the bank and the pharmacy. If one should climb to the top floor or, even better, to the roof of St. Stanislaus Church, one could see the steelworks from there. Walking along Broad Street Błażej would think: "This is where I used to take the bus, on this corner. But the guys that rode with me, they're not here no more. They went away or died." At the steel mill, Błażej had worked at sheet rolling. It took a strong man, but the pay had been good.

Just beyond the pharmacy, Broad Street rises steeply. Błażej never went past that point. He would grow short of breath, tire easily, and, anyway, why should he go there? Past that point Broad Street lost its familiar face. The city comes up from the left and gobbles it up greedily, and the hospital guards it on the right, squatting firmly, clinging to the street and barring any personal feeling, any special pacts between Błażej and Broad Street. Błażej always avoided that section of the street, though he knew that some day, helpless against the city's greed and the hospital's stony indifference, he would have to travel the whole length of the street. At the very end of Broad Street there is a cemetery. Its gravestones, half a century old, glow white from afar, if one has time to look that way in passing, when there are so many other things to look at, things far more important.

Błażej had no home, just a squalid little room in a garret. Broad Street was his home. He ruled it like a squire. He'd come to the bar at the Polish Home and say:

"Hey, you there, lock the door. I pay today. Only those I want here can come in."

On those days, if anyone Błażej did not like dared to barge in . . . with a kick in the pants, out he went. Błażej liked to fight and he was very strong. There was a man to look at! Later, when Wieniawski first met him, Błażej had changed. But one could still sense in him a tremendous strength, though now faint and subdued with age. His shoulders were still broad, but they were like two wilting leaves ready to fall with a stronger gust of wind, terribly tired of fluttering and of feigning a life that was no longer in them, though they still clung to the branch and seemed to draw its sap.

Broad Street was Błażej's home. He knew it by heart and could recognize in the dark all the uneven places on its sidewalks, all the cracks, the rough walls of the aging houses along the street, the dark hallways, and smelly courtyards. In the middle of Broad Street, where the commercial area gives way to the harbor district—to shady dives, dingy bars, and rooms for rent sheltering the scum of the city—there stands a rectangular wooden barn, an old firehouse perhaps, now turned into a food market. During the day it is full of life and the moist smells of fresh vegetables, freshly baked bread, and Polish smoked sausage. At night it becomes a shelter for tramps, where drunkards lie on the fish and meat counters until a policeman's nightstick chases them away. Błażej liked to go there and always bought something—a chicken (but only if freshly killed) or a loaf of bread—ever mindful not to overpay. To tell the truth, he would go there more to look and to talk than to buy. They knew him there.

"Ho, lookee . . . ," they would say. "Here comes Twardowski."

And the butcher would say, "Any sausage today, Twardowski?"

"Yahh," Błażej would grunt. "And how much would you want for that tiny little piece over there?" And no matter what price the butcher quoted, he would clutch his head in distress.

"All that money, all that money . . . ," he would shake his head, which, despite his age, had not a white hair on it. He refused to buy. He did not want to spend any money on himself.

"Why be so stingy, Twardowski?" they would say.

"It does me no good. I can't eat it any more," he would answer. He went to the food market to talk and to look. Others might go to a museum, to an art gallery, to the theater, or to the movies. Błażej went to Broad Street. He knew the story of every house and every store on his stretch of the street the way a museum custodian knows his exhibits.

Błażej was a conservative. He had no patience for changes and innovations. He was the first to object to Wieniawski's new office. That afternoon he picked his way down the uneven stairs of the hallway and out to St. Agnes Street, as he had daily for the past ten years, ever since he had retired from the steel mill. He stretched, yawned, and his feet carried him as if of their own will onto Broad Street.

||||

Jan Wieniawski could not get used to Broad Street. It galled and irked him, and its steep incline seemed to him a symbol of his own downhill slide. "If anyone had told me before the war that I would have to earn my living on Broad Street, I would have slapped his face or hanged myself," he often exclaimed.

To tell the truth, it was all talk and nothing else. Were it not for Broad Street, what would he do? Anyway, Wieniawski was a grumbler. He would have grumbled no matter where in the world he found himself, except, perhaps, in the old country or among understanding friends. But here he was alone, damn it, completely alone. He grumbled more to bemoan his own loneliness than anything else, and Broad Street just happened to be there to provide a handy target for his abuse. He thought it squalid, noisy, stinking, and tawdry. He deplored having to live in such degradation amid uncomprehending strangers. Wieniawski's life had begun and developed in the old country. Unlike Błażej, he talked about the old country with genuine emotion, never failing to add that it was the West and its politics that were to blame for his own forced migration to the United States. He always stressed the fact that he was a political émigré, crushed by an evil whim of fate and forced to vegetate on Broad Street, of no use to either the old country or the new.

"And those people . . . ," he sighed, thinking of the "bread immigrants" who clustered along Broad Street. "Those people . . . God have mercy! Mistrustful, suspicious, hostile. Back in Poland, I knew the peasants. Knew the workers, too. They were my people. I could always talk with them. But here . . . They are so changed in America, it is as if they have come from another planet."

He was probably right. For if Błażej represented the peasants from the old country, Wieniawski—though citified and educated over some generations—had evolved from the same stock, with unsevered bonds of deep attachment to the soil that had nurtured them both.

Both men had been washed up onto Broad Street by the waves of the bay. Błażej had accepted this philosophically, matter-of-factly, and had adapted himself and even grown fond of his new surroundings. But in Wieniawski there seethed an unending rebellion and bitterness. What would have become of him, though, were it not for Broad Street and his newly opened travel office, the Albatross?

On a warm spring afternoon filled with sun and promise, Błażej walked along St. Agnes Street, thinking he'd maybe stop at the food market, buy a chicken, and cook a pot of chicken soup to last him a week. He stopped in front of the market, shaded his eyes against the sun, looked at Broad Street . . . and blinked. He thought his eyes were failing him. He took his glasses out of his breast pocket and looked again. On the left side of the street, just past the bank, near the Polish Home, he saw a man on a ladder, painting a sign. Twardowski forgot all about his chicken. He shuffled toward the ladder, tilted his head back, and tried to make out the letters the man was painting. Failing at that, he lowered his head and looked at the freshly washed store windows in front of him.

"See that? . . ." he muttered.

There was a bilingual sign in the windows:

PACZKI DO POLSKI—PARCELS TO POLAND

"How did that happen? When?" Błażej was annoyed. Just a while ago, it seemed, there had been a hardware store here. And now? He came up closer to the windows and tried to look inside, but he couldn't see anything. Cautiously he opened the door a crack and took a look. Inside there were two men he didn't know. One was talking on the phone, and the other was sitting at a desk, writing.

"See that . . ." murmured Błażej again. He grew angry at this invasion.

"When did they come here?" he wondered.

He went on quickly to the Polish Home, pushed the door open, and hobbled along the dark corridor to the bar. He put his elbows on the counter. It had been a long time since he'd had his last beer here—the doctor had told him that he had not long to live and that drink could kill him—but they still knew him there and remembered his name.

"Those guys . . . ," he asked the barman, "Who are they?"

"What guys?"

"Over on Broad Street, in the hardware store."

"Some new people." The barman made a face. "The man's name is Wieniawski, or something like that."

"What's he doing here?" pressed Błażej.

"How would I know? I heard people say he writes letters, sends parcels to Poland."

"And if one came to him with a letter, would he read it? Can he read Polish?"

"Go and ask yourself, if you want to know."

"Not me. I don't trust that guy. Most likely all he wants is to line his pockets with other people's dollars, that's what."

For a full week Błażej circled around the store. He was upset. Were it not for the letter, he probably never would have gone inside. It was a letter from the old country, but not an ordinary one like those others that Błażej usually threw out unread, not very curious about their contents. This one was a registered letter. The mailman had brought it to Błażej and made him sign for it. The old man twirled it in his hand, considered it carefully, opened it, and tried to make out what was in it, but failed. He decided to go to the Polish Home and ask someone there to read the letter to him.

Błażej had few friends. While he was still working, while he could stand a beer or two—he'd had friends galore. But lately, more and more friends had fallen away, and those who remained had grown lukewarm.

"The beer's on me," Błażej called to the barman. "For anyone who can make out this letter."

Some came right over, bent their heads, passed the letter from hand to hand, and spelled out each word laboriously.

"It's some Gienia that is writing you, Twardowski," they concluded.

"Bolanowska?"

"Yeah."

"That's my late sister's girl. Well? What's she got to write about?"

"In the first words of my letter I advise my beloved uncle that I am alive and in good health, which is also what I wish for him . . . ."

"Stupid!" Błażej pounded the counter with his fist. "To waste all that money to write such foolishness! What else?"

"She writes that the government wants to take your land away and that it'll be necessary to go to court . . . ."

"Damn them!" Błażej rose to his feet. It suddenly came to him that he still owned a piece of land in the old country, inherited after his father's death. He never had given it a thought. Only now. That's right . . . he owned a piece of land, and now they wanted to take it away from him.

"What should I do?" He turned to the barman. "How can I save it?"

The letter, now crumpled and beer-stained, passed again from hand to hand.

"She writes she needs money to pay the lawyer."

"What can I do? What can I do?" whispered Błażej.

He looked helplessly around the dim bar, but his thoughts were far away. The land. How was he to save it? What was he to do? There was only one thought in his mind: not to give up the land, not to let it go, to keep it.

"Thieving sons of bitches, voultures, they got at me even here, they want to take my land!"

And there he was already, spread-eagled on that land, his long arms stretched out, nails dug deep in the loam, defending the land. He remembered how once, long ago, a man killed his neighbor because he had plowed over his path. Even kinship did not matter. For land, a man would crack his brother's skull wide open. And those strangers aimed to take his land. His own land, his patrimony.

"What should I do?" he moaned. "How can I save it?" He never stopped to think why or for whom he should be trying to save that piece of land that he had never wanted to see again, that surely he would never see again. He felt as if someone were tearing out his vitals, slicing his belly open, and murdering him. He was fighting for his very life—for land. His legs trembled, and his body felt clammy with sweat.

"What should I do? Tell me what to do."

"Why don't you try and talk to Wieniawski about it? Maybe he can help."

"Give me back my letter."

He smoothed out the sheets, folded the letter, slipped it into its envelope, and without further ado went to Wieniawski's office to seek help.

|||

Stefański the organist jumped up from behind his desk.

"What's the matter with you? Are you coming in or not? It must be a dozen times you've opened that door."

Hesitant, Błażej stood in the doorway, looking the place over.

"I want to see the one who can send money to the old country."

"Which one? Perhaps I can help you?"

Błażej walked in. He looked at Stefański suspiciously.

"You wouldn't be Wieniawski, would you?"

"No," said the organist. "If you want to see Mr. Wieniawski you'll have to wait."

"A miser," he thought. "I know the kind. I won't make a buck off him, anyway. If he wants to wait for Wieniawski, so much the better."

Błażej took no offense. Slowly, he began to feel a bit more sure of himself. Crossing the threshold had been the worst of it. "I know that man from somewheres," he thought, looking at Stefański bent over the papers on his desk.

"You're just from the old country?"

The organist gave a start. "Why?"

"Nothing. Just thought maybe you came over a short while ago."

"It shows, huh? Do I look different?"

"You talk different. Where did you come from?"

"Warsaw." He sighed. "Just sit there and wait. I'm busy."

Błażej turned away, but he did not sit down. He was standing against the map on the wall, his shoulders hunched, his hand exploring his pocket to see if the letter was still there.

"When did you come over here?"

"Anything else you'd like to know? Why don't you mind your own business?"

"Seems to me like you must be that new organist over at St. Agnes . . . ."

"So what?"

"Nothing. Heard people say he came over recently."

"Can't you stop talking? I got work to do."

The truth was that Stefański—the Party's prize pupil, the pride of the People's Republic, the flower of the new communist elite, the respected and admired official—had chosen freedom.

Błażej took out a half-smoked cigar, stuck it between his false teeth, smacked his lips, and lit it up.

"Well, then . . . How are things over there now?"

Stefański looked at him with bloodshot eyes. "Can't you see I'm working? How can they be? Bad."

"It's better over here?"

"If only I could, I'd go back. I'd just as soon leave the United States. What sort of life can one have here? . . ."

Wieniawski walked in briskly. "You want to see me?" He glanced at Błażej. "Just a moment, I'll be right with you. One second."

Without taking off his coat, he went inside, behind a plywood partition that separated the attorney's office.

"Where is Dekrocki?" he called out. "Mr. Stefański, hasn't Dekrocki been here at all?"

"No, sir, he hasn't been here today."

"Where in blazes does he keep himself? Why doesn't he mind the shop?"

Hanging up his hat and coat and inveighing loudly, Wieniawski turned an angry red.

"That's the American sense of duty for you, that's the kind of responsibility . . . ."

A shadow loomed up behind him—the organist was bigger and taller than Wieniawski—and leaned over him: "Mr. Wieniawski . . . sh . . . sh . . . sh . . . you're talking too much and too loudly. No use cursing. The walls have ears . . . ."

"There you go again, Mr. Stefański. I've told you time and again that it's a free country here."

"I have already heard . . . I'm warning you as a friend. Anyway, do you know who that man may be? That one, over there, the one who's been waiting for you?"

"Mr. Stefański, over here we are . . . ," began Wieniawski. But then he changed his mind and only shrugged.

"The client . . . that's right," he said. "I'm coming right away."

"I can wait," said Błażej. He took the letter from his pocket, smoothed it out with the back of his hand. "Bastards," he muttered, "Damned vooltures . . . ."

"What can I do for you?" Błażej's tired face seemed gray behind the screen of his cigar smoke. He hid behind it. Wieniawski looked at him closely—and saw nothing but the eyes of the stranger, two headlights of a car lost in the fog.

"An old-timer," thought Wieniawski. "He wants to send a parcel to the old country."

Safe behind his cigar, yet lost in the smoke screen, Błażej appraised the man before him. "Who's he like?" he thought. "He reminds me of someone . . . ." But there had been too many people in Błażej's long life to remember, and it was too tiresome to think.

"Can you read a letter in Polish?" he asked suspiciously.

"Sure."

"And how much would you want for reading it?"

"For reading a letter?" Wieniawski was surprised. "Nothing."

A spring afternoon was marching up Broad Street from the bay. It did not smell of leaves and freshly turned soil, but of fish from the market stalls and humid wind. Swatches of sun lay on the sidewalk outside the travel office windows. Once more, Błażej smoothed the letter with the back of his hand, as if wanting to erase the beer stains. Reluctantly, warily, he pushed the letter toward Wieniawski. And immediately he moved his big body and leaned over to watch intently while Wieniawski was reading the letter, scanning his face suspiciously all the while.

"Well, what is it she wants?" he asked at last. "Why is she writing?" he asked, even though he knew already what was in the letter. "Can you read it? Can you make it out?"

Wieniawski looked up.

"She writes that the government wants to take over that piece of land you inherited from your father; they want to take it over for the state . . . ."

"I know that. What else?"

"If you know, then why . . . ."

A gust of wind blew through the suddenly opened door. Attorney Dekrocki walked in. "It's high time you showed up, Antek," called Wieniawski. "You were to be in court at one o'clock, That's a fine way to act."

Dekrocki was a jovial man, fond of a good meal like the one he had just finished.

"Never mind," he muttered.

"My respects, sir," bowed Stefański.

Dekrocki made his way past Błażej and around Stefański.

"Blowing like the dickens out there," he said, "On the corner it nearly blew me off my feet." He went behind the partition. Błażej moved uneasily.

"What else does it say there?" he pressed.

"If you already know, why do you ask?"

"Go on, read it, don't get your dander up. But we must hurry, I need your advice!"

"About what?"

"So they won't take that land away."

"Well, let's see now," mused Wieniawski. "We could save it, I suppose, if you ceded your rights to your niece."

"To Gienia?"

"That's right. To Gienia. She writes that we have ten days in which to do something. We would have to go to the embassy right away and certify that you made a gift of that land to Gienia. Then we'd have to wire her one hundred dollars, like she says."

"How much will all this come to?" fretted Błażej.

"Of course, there'll be some additional expenses. But perhaps you don't want to give that land to your niece? Not that you'll ever have any use for . . . ."

Błażej smiled craftily, an inward smile stretched his lips. He was taut and tense. His feet tingled. "Won't give it to any strangers," he said. "It's better to let Gienia have it. But we must hurry or they'll take it away from us. Let's hurry!" He spoke excitedly.

He got up and paced back and forth, puffing impatiently on his cigar. Now Wieniawski could take a good look at him. The old man was powerfully built but worn with age. His head drooped to one side, as if it were too heavy for the neck that supported it. Wieniawski looked at him thoughtfully.

"How old are you, may I ask?"

"About seventy-eight. Why?"

Wieniawski said nothing. "He could be my father," he thought, and felt a twinge of a forgotten emotion. It had been many years since his father had died.

"A handsome age," he said aloud. "Do you have any children, either here or in Poland?"

"I have no one."

"And that . . . Gienia Bolanowska?"

"That's my late sister's girl."

Wieniawski pulled out a sheet of paper and began to prepare an act of donation. Błażej, meanwhile, put on his glasses, reached for the letter again, and strained once more to figure out its contents.

"What does it say here?" He pointed with his finger.

"I thought you knew what the letter says."

"No, over here. Start reading from here, please."

His work on Broad Street had taught Wieniawski patience. He smoothed out the crumpled sheets and began reading aloud:

Dear Uncle,

I had a joy once in my life I'll never have again. I have to describe it to you. My husband and me, we were driving back from Zierańsk and saw a man walking from the bus, from Wronki, because now one can get to Wronki by bus. So I told my husband to stop the horse and wait for that man. He came near us and I asked him directly where he was going, and he said he was going to the Wołuskis, and he was beautifully dressed and a tall, good-looking man, like Godzianowska once told me you were, so I thought it was you and asked who he was going to visit at the Wołuskis, and he asked if there was a family there by the name of Bolanowski. So I could not hold my joy any more and I jumped down from the cart and said, ah, perhaps you are my beloved uncle from America . . . .

"That's what she says?" Błażej asked dubiously. "She's dumb," he laughed, but his eyes were moist.

Wieniawski went on reading.

He just laughed and said no, he was not, and I burst out crying because he was making fun of me, and he asked why hadn't I recognized him, surely I must have had my uncle's picture, and yet made such a mistake. And I said no, I don't have my uncle's picture and know him only from what others who knew him told me. And he said, you probably love your uncle very much if you are so anxious to see him. And I said, you know, he is a father and a mother to me, because I have no one but the Good Lord and him . . . .

"Is that right? That's what she says?" murmured Błażej. "Then I'll send her fifty dollars extra and have a picture taken for her," he promised.

Wieniawski's office filled with cigar smoke. Błażej walked back and forth in it as in a fog. He rose high, floated effortlessly, and descended on the road leading from Wronki to the bus station. . . . That's my beloved uncle, my father and my mother to me, I am trying to save his land for him, so he can come here when he is older . . . Land . . . land . . .

"Do you have any money with you, Mr. Twardowski?"

Błażej came to and cast a sharp look.

"Sure I do. But I won't give you any money," he told Wieniawski. And, seeing the surprise on Wieniawski's face, he added: "I won't. I don't trust you."

"Well then, how . . . ." shrugged Wieniawski.

"I'll give it to that lawyer fellow."

"Antek!" called Wieniawski. "Please come here and take the money from our client."

That was all he said. But he was upset. Something he thought he had re-captured turned out to be an illusion after all. Błażej was counting out the money stolidly, handing it over to Dekrocki. Stefański looked on with interest. The four of them, all with last names ending in "ski," were now gathered in the front room of the office. Twardowski, the eldest of them, had come to America half a century before. Dekrocki had been born here. Wieniawski was a political immigrant: he had come after World War II. And Stefański, raised in communist postwar Poland, had chosen freedom. Yet here they were, all together, all Poles.

Błażej was counting out his money: "Twenty dollars . . . forty dollars . . . ."

The next day, Wieniawski would send it off special delivery to the old country in a last-ditch effort to save a small piece of land. But to save it for whom? Neither he nor Błażej would ever till that land. And yet to both it now seemed more real, more beloved than friendly Broad Street, beaming with the warmth of the afternoon sun.

||I

It was as if they had waited for that first signal, the first homeward flight of a homing pigeon, as if they had been huddling forever behind a door left slightly ajar, cold and hungry, greedy, empty-bellied, they and their children, and their cows and horses, and their dilapidated barns and sheds. It was as if, pushing each other away and yet supporting each other, they had been scanning the sky, awaiting the return of that first daring and fortunate messenger. It was scarcely a few weeks after Gienia had received Błażej's money that a flood of letters poured in.

All Błażej's cousins and relatives from the old country descended upon him through letters written on lined sheets of paper enclosed in blue envelopes. No one would entrust his message to regular mail. All letters were registered or registered air mail. Those who had never taken a pen in hand since their school days now reached for this mighty weapon. Their letters bore traces of corrections made by teachers or by youngsters fresh out of school. They came in a flood. The first to arrive was a letter from Błażej's stepbrother, Konstanty Pazdruk:

> My Dear Brother,
> I write you these few words with sorrow in my heart and tears in my eyes, because I know nothing about your life and health, because I don't know what has happened, why you will not deign to answer my letter. Dear brother, I lost my horse and now have to pull the plow myself, with the help of my son . . . .

Błażej listened attentively. He scratched his head and looked at Wieniawski.

"I guess we should send him some money to buy a new horse," he said. "He's not really my brother, but a brother still."

"How much?" asked Wieniawski. By then it was summer; the office door was left wide open onto the street, and waves of heat rose low above the sidewalk.

"Send him one hundred dollars."

Błażej took the money out of his pocket and laid it on Wieniawski's desk. They looked at each other. Błażej was shy, apologetic. Wieniawski was disbelieving, but smiled. After Błażej learned that the first money sent to the old country had arrived there in good time, he had begun to trust Wieniawski. Perhaps there was even something more there: the first stirrings of some still undefined liking.

"One hundred dollars?" asked Wieniawski solicitously. "Are you sure you can afford that much?"

"Yes. I got my monthly retirement from the steel mill, and the government pays me Social Security."

Wieniawski asked no more. He thought, "Probably he has some savings, too." But he knew that the subject of savings was taboo. Broad Street people never talked about their savings. They trusted no one when it came to that. They never talked about themselves, either. They were taciturn and stubborn. Wieniawski knew so little about Błażej.

Konstanty wrote back promptly.

My Dear Brother,
My son got married now and he took the horse away, and I can't pull the plow all by myself. They plague us with taxes here till a man can't stand it anymore. The young ones abandon their land, they run away to factories, and, weak as I am, I must toil, my youth gone, old age upon me. If it weren't for you, my dear brother, and your help, I don't know how I would manage . . . .

"Well," said Błażej. "Send him a hundred dollars, so he can buy himself a new horse."

Błażej's stepbrother Konstanty acquired such a taste for writing that hardly a month went by without a new letter being sent off to America. But that wasn't the end of it. The three children of Błażej's late sister—Gienia, Józek, and Stanisław—did not spare ink or postage for registered letters either. Stanisław wrote:

Dear Uncle,
In the first words of my letter, I, Stanisław, wish you health, because good health is the most precious thing in a man's life. Dear Uncle, I, Stanisław, son of Józio, am turning to you for help. I know that you're no longer working, because your working years are over, but you helped Gienia and Wikta and Józek, so I would also like to have something to remember you by, and now it would come in handy, because I lost my cow this past year and my wife's health isn't good. I have three children, the oldest one is six, and I must do everything myself, and my barn fell down and

I must put it up again, because I have no place to store my wheat, though I put up hay in a stack, but even a few pennies for a carpenter, if you could send them, would be of great help, and I will pray that the Good Lord grant you good health. To meet my payments I had to sell two cows and my last mare and I have now only one cow, one pig, and two piglets. Dear Uncle, I send you my best greetings, and so does my family, too, and wish you good health, and please answer my letter and do not refuse my request.

I remain,

Your loving nephew,

Stanisław

Five months had gone by since Błażej first sent Gienia the money to fight for their land in the courts. It was late summer, the end of August. The heat of the day swirled in humid knots over Broad Street, and the midday sun burned with a pale, cruel flame in the narrow corridor of the sky above. In the countryside, farmers began to pick the corn. Red dust followed their tractors. A breeze from the north, from the mountains, would sometimes pass its cool hand over their sweaty faces. But there, in the bowl of the bay, the stagnant air lay heavy, trembling, and weary. Błażej had gotten used to this climate, and his long years at the steel mill had taught him to cope with heat. Dekrocki had gone north to the lakes on vacation. The organist Stefański came in rarely: the heat bothered him so much that he spent his days lying prostrate on his bed, barely conscious until nightfall, turning this way and that in front of a fan and longing for the more bearable climate of the old country. Only Wieniawski remained at his desk in the Albatross Travel Office.

It had been a long time since Błażej had felt as chipper as he did now. He dropped in at the Albatross more and more often, without even noticing that he had become a daily guest there. He and Wieniawski would sip an ice-cold Coca-Cola together or, for variety, a cup of hot coffee, with which they were better able to beat the heat. They had a great deal to talk about. Requests for help kept flowing in from more and more relatives. For instance, there was a letter from Konstanty's daughter:

I haven't got any money yet. I'm waiting for your answer. Father tells me: "Be patient, he'll help you. You, my daughter, must remember that you have a kindhearted uncle who cares about his family and you must repay him some day in the future." So, I beg you, my Dear Uncle, to help me, if

you are able, and to lighten my burden. Please answer me soon. I remain in
sorrow and longing, me and my whole family.

All the letters brought thanks and blessings, requests for advice, tales of
troubles, and invitations to the old country. Józek (whom Błażej described to
Wieniawski as "the learned one who holds an office") was the most cordial in
his invitations:

> You could write me a few words, my Dear Uncle, to let me know about
> your health and to answer my questions from my previous letters. You did
> mention once the possibility of your coming to Poland to visit your home-
> land with a view of remaining there in your later years, but we have heard
> nothing more about this subject. Personally, in the event such plans come to
> pass, I would fully expect to render you all the assistance in my power—as
> would my wife—and to take care of you, Dear Uncle, in your old age. God
> forbid, Dear Uncle, that you should think I was motivated by thoughts of
> personal profit in this undertaking. Rather, I would do it out of the fullness
> of my heart and in all sincerity, as I would for my own parents were they
> still alive. It is my heartfelt desire, Dear Uncle, to hear from you regarding
> the questions I outlined in this letter. In closing, I am sending you my best
> and most loving regards and best wishes from your loving nephew Józek,
> his wife, daughter, and son.

Wikta also invited Błażej to come to the old country:

> If the Good Lord permits, I shall see you here, my Dear Uncle, since my
> father says that come spring you will probably travel our way. Dear Uncle,
> with this money I would like to do something for myself and for the chil-
> dren, so they will always remember you. Please advise me what I should do.
> I would like to build my own house, because we are living now in a very
> small apartment. But I can't build a house without your help, because we
> have a hard time here getting the building materials, but you can get every-
> thing from the bank if you pay in dollars. Dear Uncle, if you could send me
> another hundred dollars, I won't touch the other hundred, but use the en-
> tire two hundred dollars to buy bricks, and that should be enough for a
> small house. . . .

"Why don't you go to Poland, since they invite you so cordially?"
asked Wieniawski.

Błażej smiled.

"I thought once maybe I would," he said. "But I couldn't survive such a trip."

|||

Each morning he dragged himself, wet with sweat, from the pallet in his room on St. Agnes Street. He turned back his sheet, the only one he had, and spread it in the sun to dry. He then ate some chicken soup straight from the pot and a slice of bread and went out to see Wieniawski, to chat or to send off more money. He was happy. Only one thing bothered him: he had no word from Gienia about his case in court.

"Did they lose? What happened?" he fretted. Yet his good mood persisted. Now he had something to do each day, something to look forward to, someone to see and talk to. He would sit on a chair in the corner of the office and listen to Wieniawski's conversations with his clients. This was of great interest to him, because many people returning from Poland would stop at the Albatross and share their stories with Wieniawski.

One morning he came to the office in a more cheerful mood than usual. He felt young, boisterous, almost as strong as in those old days when he had drunkenly "put Moscow to rout." He could no longer remember what it was that had made him angry enough to rush over to where the Russian emigrants lived and destroy their homes. They had put him in jail, and when he got out he never again tried anything like that, but he had gained a reputation as someone to be reckoned with. Something like a fleeting reflection of that same old feeling was with him as he walked up Broad Street to the Albatross that morning, humming a tune. He sang

> Poor old mother did not know
> How to call her son-in-law.
> "Get up, get up, you lazy bum.
> "Get out and plow the field."

Then he sang

> She fell from a cherry tree, we all saw it . . . .

And finally, at the door of the Albatross, he sang softly

He told me he would take me, would take me,
As soon as he harvested his field.
But the harvest's over, the sheaves are all tied,
And my own world is all tied up, too.
He came to me all winter, all winter,
I let him warm himself under my feather bed . . . .

From the threshold Błażej waved a blue banner, another letter, at Wieniawski.

"Again a letter for more money," he called cheerily.

But Wieniawski did not laugh back as usual.

"One moment, Mr. Twardowski," he said. "Let me take care of these people here first."

Only then did Błażej notice that there were two people in Wieniawski's office. Across the desk from Wieniawski, the chair creaked under a little rotund lady with a homely face and bright eyes under a beflowered hat brim. His attention was drawn immediately to her legs. They were swollen, massive, like church pillars, even larger than Błażej's, big man that he was.

He glanced sidelong at the woman's earrings, at her profile reflected in the front window, and knew who she was: Mrs. Roguska. He lowered himself into his chair in the corner, took a cigar from the breast pocket of his jacket, and eavesdropped contentedly.

"Are you pleased with your trip?" asked Wieniawski.

"You know how it is. Everything was fine. But I should have taken a fan with me."

A man sitting at the other end of the room cleared his throat. He was neatly dressed in a Sunday suit, white haired, with a face like a freshly plowed spring field.

"A fan?" Wieniawski asked, puzzled.

All three men leaned in curiously toward Mrs. Roguska. Her huge legs did not shift. Only her face changed, showing hints of a smile, and her earlobe jumped—hop! hop!—under the weight of her earring, which itself dangled like a tiny bell.

"You see, sir, over there, when you go behind a barn and squat down, there are always wasps. You need a fan to shoo them off, damn it, so they don't bite."

The men chuckled appreciatively. But Roguska's face remained placid.

"If you go to Poland, take a fan with you, I say. And some good American dollars."

The white-haired man got up. Standing up, he seemed younger.

"And I say, dollars and toilet paper. You can't get any there. I tried once, and what they gave me wouldn't be enough for a bird. So I thought to myself: what'll I do? Well, I took a ten-zloty bill and used it. But later on a young lady in a store told me to buy a calendar. She said all foreigners buy calendars; it's good paper, she said. So, if you ask me, I say: don't go without toilet paper, because you can't get any for love or money."

Błażej laughed so hard his cigar fell out of his mouth. But this soon changed to a rasping, painful cough. It was embarrassing. Everybody looked at him, and Wieniawski called:

"What's the matter, Błażej? Want a glass of water?"

"Nahh . . . ," he waved Wieniawski off. "Never mind. Coffee . . . I'll get some coffee."

He went out, perturbed, and before going to the Polish Home for coffee he went walking along Broad Street, whose kindly noise covered up the hollow, hacking sound of his coughing. Only when everything within him had quieted down did he shuffle over to the Polish Home. Spent and tired, he pushed open the door of the restaurant.

"Two coffees for me," he said. When he returned to the Albatross carrying paper cups in both hands, Wieniawski's two visitors were gone. Błażej put one cup on Wieniawski's desk and sipped slowly from the other.

"Thank you, Mr. Twardowski. Here's a dime for the coffee."

Błażej shook his head.

"Never mind. You keep it."

Wieniawski was surprised. Błażej did not like to spend money. He lived like a pauper, begrudging himself everything, even food. Sometimes he would splurge and spend a quarter for a bowl of soup, but usually he cooked himself a pot of chicken soup to last him a long while. Was it possible, Wieniawski wondered, that Błażej was sending all his money to Poland? Was it possible that, after all those years at the steel mill, he had no savings? Błażej had bought him a cup of coffee. Incredible! Was this perhaps his way of repaying Wieniawski for reading all those letters to him or for answering them for him? Or was there another explanation for the treat? Could it be, simply, that Błażej had grown . . . to like him? That the distrustful loner, the coarse peasant felt he had something in common with Wieniawski? Was this a show of confidence, the beginning of a friendship? Wieniawski slipped the dime back in his pocket, but he felt that he had been given much more than a dime. Somehow he felt in debt.

Meanwhile, Błażej pulled another letter from his ample pockets. This one was from his stepbrother Konstanty.

"What's in there?" asked Błażej. "What is it this time?" Wieniawski read:

My Dear Brother,
    With the first words of this letter . . . may our Lord be praised. There are so many needs, the roof is caving in, misery waits on the threshold . . . .

Wieniawski stopped reading. He looked at Błażej. "Should I tell him?" he thought. "I'll tell him," he decided. "But then he won't send any more money. I won't get my commission." He hesitated, but only briefly. "I can't do that. That man trusts me. I'll tell him."

Suspecting nothing, guileless, Błażej urged Wieniawski: "Go on, read it to me."

"Well," said Wieniawski brusquely, startled at the sound of his own voice—"Why do I take it to heart so? What for?"—"There is some more here about the taxes and that he gave an offering to have a Mass said for you . . . ."

"He had a Mass said for me?" Błażej was delighted. "He did? All right then, you write him: Here is another hundred for you . . . ." He broke off to check whether Wieniawski was taking down every word, " . . . and another hundred for the parish priest to make repairs on that leaking church roof you wrote me about." He smiled again. "And write him to stop that misery right there on the threshold, don't let him in. And then . . . ," he stopped to think. "That parish priest . . . would that be Jasiek Lipa?"

"Jasiek Lipa?"

"Jasiek Lipa," said Błażej. He looked at Wieniawski expectantly, as if awaiting a confirmation.

"How would I know?" shrugged Wieniawski. He was thinking: "I won't tell him. Let him find out for himself." And then: "How can I not tell him? He trusts me."

Błażej kept looking at him, waiting.

"Who is Jasiek Lipa?" asked Wieniawski finally.

It was as if Twardowski had been waiting for just that. He seated himself comfortably, stretched out his legs, and began his tale. After his father's death, when his mother got married again, things had been tough for him. He never had enough to eat, he tended the cows, and he had a chip on his shoulder— there was no one in this world he liked. That Jasiek Lipa, he hadn't liked him either. He was so smart, so learned, and yet somehow Jasiek Lipa knew how to draw close to Błażej, how to make a friend of him. He taught him to read and write. They would often sit together just talking . . . the old man hesitated. "Just as we do now," he said, "And yet he was smarter than you. He could understand everything. We became friends."

Wieniawski's burden seemed heavier with Błażej's every word. The old man's confidences disturbed him, but he dared not rebuff him. "I'll tell him," he decided. "So what if he doesn't send them another cent? The man trusts me, I can't deceive him."

"Błażej . . . ," he began carefully, as if he were stepping into a stream, afraid of each step, fearful of muddying the clear water and pulling in the other man, too. "You've been asking me how come Gienia doesn't write anything about that court action you sent money for, and what's happened to your land."

"Well?" said Błażej. His face grew taut. He leaned forward. "Well?"

Wieniawski reached into a drawer and fished out a large white envelope, addressed on a typewriter. He took out a sheet of paper covered with even, typewritten rows of letters. Błażej kept still.

"From the court?" he whispered.

"From a lawyer."

"Did they give back the land?"

"You see, I wrote to the nearest attorney there in Poland, in a neighboring town. I asked him to find out all he could about your case. You've been waiting so long and have sent so much money already . . . ."

"Did they win?" he whispered through a constricted throat, "Did they win? Did they give the land back to her?"

"There was no trial."

"Not yet? When?"

"Never."

"Why not?" There was a note of alarm in his voice. "Too little money? I sent her three hundred dollars and then another hundred. That's not enough?"

"The lawyer writes something about . . . let's see . . . about prescription."

"How's that?"

"Here, see for yourself." Wieniawski pushed the letter toward Błażej. "Look here . . . ."

Błażej pushed the letter away impatiently. "You read it to me. You tell me . . . ."

"You see, the man who occupies that land now, some cousin or distant relation, has a claim on it by prescription, because of a long and continued use. That's what that lawyer writes."

"That stranger has a right to my land?"

"Yes, because of the length of time he has held it. There was no trial and there won't be any. No one knows anything about it. Gienia simply fooled you. Obviously . . . What is the matter, Twardowski? What is it? Błażej?"

The old man's face was scarlet. His hair shone white against his red forehead. He got to his feet, faltered, fell back into his chair, and breathed heavily. He tried to rise again, but the floor seemed to give way under his feet, as if it were that faraway land over there, in the old country, as if, unknowing, he had been walking all along on that land and now found out it was no longer there to support him, no longer his.

"She cheated me . . . ," he groaned.

There was such despair in his voice, such cruel disappointment, that Wieniawski shuddered. All his own forgotten sorrows returned, and old longings rose up, appearing before him like a legion of ghosts called to muster, staring at him through dead eyes.

"They cheated us," he sorrowed. "They cheated us. Now we have no land."

Błażej was the first to recover himself. He grabbed the edge of Wieniawski's desk and half raised himself, but did not fully straighten up. Something had broken in him, some light had gone out, but his muffled voice had regained a measure of strength and, with it, bitterness.

"She cheated me. They all cheated me, the vooltures. You write to my nephew Stanisław right away: I don't want to know you! I want nothing to do with you any more. Not any of you."

Then he turned and left without saying good-bye. Wieniawski watched him shuffle along Broad Street. He looked old and weary.

"Damn it!" muttered Wieniawski. "I've lost a client." But he knew well enough that that was not why he was swearing. That was not what troubled him at all.

III

"I haven't seen Twardowski in here these last few days," said Stefański, the organist.

"No, he hasn't been here," scowled Wieniawski.

"There's no one to bring us coffee now."

"Can't you get off your ass and bring it yourself?"

Stefański smiled. "You're really taking this to heart, I see. They swindled him, those people over there, didn't they? They wheedled dollars out of him under false pretenses. Let me tell you—they're all bastards, every one of them. Let them fight it out among themselves." He grew agitated. "Let me tell you—they're not worth a damn! I know them. For a dollar, they'd hack one another to pieces. Well, let them. Good riddance!"

"It's your own people you're talking about."

"I'm talking about the communists. What's with you? Are you on their side?"

"I won't spit on my own people. I wasn't raised by the communists. I got nothing from them. You got everything. Let me tell you something, Mr. Stefański: you are an unhappy man. I feel sorry for you. I feel more sorry for you than for those people over there or for those here, for that matter."

Stefański did not answer. He listened to a far-off echo within himself, a painful dissonance of love and hate, admiration and contempt, subdued by an overwhelming fear. It all seemed too difficult. And yet there had been a time when nothing seemed too difficult for him. Only church walls could weather such a storm of dissonant feelings. The human skull was too fragile, too small to withstand the pressure. And yet Stefański was an intelligent man, a good man, a man of sensibilities. His fingers could cajole the keys, playing unerring, instinctive pianissimos.

"I have a headache," he mumbled finally.

"Take an aspirin."

"A fat lot of good an aspirin will do me. I get a headache and everything just churns inside me whenever you talk to me like that. All right, tell me: is it my fault?"

Twardowski was walking slowly along St. Agnes Street toward Broad Street. For the past few days he had stayed in his room, fighting a severe asthma attack. Now he felt better. Only his face looked thinner and tired. He dragged his feet as he walked, and he breathed with effort.

He went to the Albatross and pushed the door open. He never stopped to think why. He just went. He'd gotten used to going there. Where else was he to go? Had anyone ever invited him any place?

Wieniawski was glad to see him. "Well, how have you been, Mr. Twardowski?"

"I'll bring some coffee," Błażej muttered.

When he got back, he sat down in his old chair against the wall. He said nothing. It felt good just to sit there.

Wieniawski felt some pangs of conscience. He felt somehow responsible, as if he had been derelict in taking care of the old man. He had earned a commission for his services, taking the old man's money, and it might have seemed that that was the only link between them. But now that their business relationship had come to an end, now that Wieniawski had fulfilled whatever reasonable expectations Błażej could have had, Wieniawski felt as if this were the beginning rather than the end of their relationship. He felt somehow in debt, and it irked him. He thought: "I have no time for this, I've got to work. No one's going to pay me any retirement, I don't have any Social Security coming, and here he sits on his backside and bothers me." Aloud he said: "Have a seat, Mr. Twardowski. Tell me what's new?"

Wieniawski was a practical man, a realist who put high value on time and money. But he also felt strongly about what he called "an honest approach to business." This was a feeling that had been ingrained in him many years earlier, before he ever thought he would be pronouncing the word "business" the way English-speaking people do. And it was probably this feeling, stronger than Wieniawski's high regard for time and a practical approach to life, that made him say, "Have a seat, Mr. Twardowski." And something else, too, perhaps some vague, gnawing feeling of guilt.

"How's that?" Błażej scraped the floor with his chair, moving it closer to Wieniawski's desk.

"I'll be going now," said Stefański.

"Tomorrow, as usual."

"All right. Good-bye."

Stefański turned back in the doorway. "I forgot. Mrs. Sójka called."

"Good grief! You never told me."

"Well, you pounced on me so . . . ."

"Don't you know me by now? I say what I think."

"That's not what I mean. In fact, I like it better that way. Others would be thinking and never saying what's on their mind. But still, a man's not made of steel."

"I disagree with you," said Wieniawski. "I think perhaps all men are made of steel. But not all steel is equally well tempered. Well, what did Mrs. Sójka want now?"

"It's still that business about finding a wife for her son. She said she'd call again or come over. She called when you were out to lunch. Good-bye!"

"Good-bye."

Błażej looked from one to the other. What were they talking about? Was there a squabble? If need be, he felt he would take Wieniawski's side. He had defended him once already at the Polish Home.

"Don't go to Wieniawski," he'd heard people say. "Don't support his business. He's a stuck-up landlord son of a bitch."

Błażej had answered: "Shame on you, talking such garbage. He's no landowner, just an educated man, that's all."

And when they jeered, he was ready to fight. And although he was weak now, they remembered his huge strength and stopped yapping.

"Watch out!" they had only laughed. "That's the guy who fought Moscow."

"You see, Mr. Twardowski," began Wieniawski. "I think a rest would do you a world of good. You should get away somewhere. Relax, rest, rebuild your strength . . . ."

"Baloney," Błażej snorted angrily. "It would cost money."

"But you have your retirement, your Social Security."

"No sense even talking about it," Twardowski flared up.

Now Wieniawski raised his voice, too. He was annoyed.

"What are you saving your money for?" he said, talking to all the Twardowskis, to all Broad Street. "What are you all skimping for? Damned if I can understand it. You'll all go to the devil, and then the state will get its hands on your money." Błażej started.

"You say the state will take the money?"

"Of course. Don't I hear enough about it? A man goes on all his life scrimping, saving, denying himself every comfort. Then one fine day he dies, he has no family, and the state gets everything."

"But I have nowhere to go."

"Don't you have any relatives in the States?"

"No."

"How about that woman Konstanty mentioned in his letter? That cousin in Pittsburgh?"

"Frances?"

"That's it. How closely related are you?"

"Her mother and my stepfather's father were . . . ."

"Never mind. But she is related to you?"

"I don't know her. I wouldn't go there, anyway, because, I tell you . . . ," he lowered his voice, "I won't live much longer."

"Nonsense!" cried Wieniawski indignantly.

"This year is my last year. A doctor told me long ago. And that thing with Gienia, I thought it would be the end of me."

"That's just silly talk, Błażej. Gienia is stupid and greedy, her husband is dying of TB. She has small children. Still, of course, she shouldn't have . . . ."

"She cheated me. I won't have anything to do with her. But you said the state will take all my money?"

"It will, unless you have a will. But why should you worry about it? You don't have to save and probably can't save much anyway."

"Mr. Wieniawski . . . ," Błażej began in a low voice, but stopped because the door flew open and a scrawny old woman burst in so impetuously that all the windows rattled and all the papers on Wieniawski's desk flew every which way. She was shouting from the threshold:

"I've got a stupid husband and a stupid son, Mr. Wieniawski. They went to the old country to get our boy married, they've been gone one month already, they took money with them—and nothing. And here I am, barely able to move, with everything to do by myself, and have to think for these two stupid oafs, too."

"Calm down, Mrs. Sójka," said Wieniawski. "It's not so easy to find a good wife. What does your husband write?"

Mrs. Sójka glared at Błażej, who retreated to the far end of the office but listened eagerly.

"Well, he writes, they are both in the village, they are spending my money, but that the girls there are not much in touching."

"What do you mean, 'in touching'?"

"How would I know? That's my curse, that I have a stupid husband and a stupid son. You can look for yourself. Here. He says everything is all right, but that the girls are not much in touching."

"He probably wants to find one that is pretty, and a good worker, and without a baby."

"How would I know what he wants? He's dumb, that's all. They took five hundred dollars with them and they'll come back without a wife. My feet are giving me trouble—rheumatism, you know—I've got to have a young woman in the house."

Błażej had stopped listening. He was thinking about Frances. Should he perhaps write her? He remembered her mother, Bogula. He recalled her dimly, standing in front of the house, and in the back of the house there was a pear tree. He remembered clearly the tart taste of the pears and their coarse brown skin. In his mind, it was somehow associated with a feeling of fright mixed with gratitude. It was strange how clearly it came back to him. He remembered how one evening he had sneaked behind the house to pick some pears. He had gotten well up in the tree when he heard her voice: "Is that you there, Błażek?" He had grown faint with fear. What now? She would chase him away, sic a dog on him, complain to his stepfather? "Is that you, Błażek?"

"Yes,'" he had whispered, "But I didn't mean to . . . ."

"Pick yourself some pears," she had told him, "But mind you don't break the branches. And don't eat too many. They're not ripe yet."

He couldn't believe his own ears. What had happened? She hadn't chased or scolded him. He had been so overwhelmed with gratitude that he hadn't even picked any pears. And now in a dark corner of the office, hidden behind Dekrocki's law books, lonely, he cried for that long-past day, for that generosity, and, perhaps, out of longing for the Błażej of long ago. For that one had been a boy of fire and hope, resolute and unyielding.

"You are so smart, Błażek," Jasiek Lipa had marveled. "You should go to school. You'll go far."

"Who knows?" Błażek had answered, "Maybe I will."

"You know what?" Jasiek had said, "If you have a son, make him study to be a priest or a teacher. Spare no money. I'll help him. I'll teach him and guide him," he promised. "He'll be a priest or a doctor or an engineer. He'll be an educated man. But it takes money."

Now that he was old and sick and lonely, Twardowski missed the young

Błażek and the tart taste of hard pears. He had money, it was true, but he had no son.

"I'll tell Wieniawski to write to Frances," he decided. And right away he felt much better, because he remembered that Konstanty had written that Frances, Bogula's daughter, had a young son.

Later on Wieniawski would chide himself: "It was all my own doing. I pointed him in that direction. And now look at all the trouble I have made for myself."

But by then it was too late. A letter went to Frances in Pittsburgh, and before Christmas Frances wrote back to her "Dear Cousin" with an invitation to come and stay at her home for the holidays. Wieniawski translated the letter faithfully, word for word, just as he had the letters that came from the old country, but Błażej paid no attention to those now. Just before he left for Pittsburgh, though, he softened a bit and brought some of them to Wieniawski's office to be read.

Konstanty wrote: "I managed to keep the wolves away and fixed the roof, but now my horse went lame . . . ."

In Wieniawski's hand, Błażej wrote back: "Here is another hundred dollars for you and, blast it, leave me alone!"

And Konstanty's youngest daughter wrote that she had no decent dress to wear, so she couldn't go to church. But Błażej only laughed.

"The scum! Vooltures! When I tended my cows I had no pants to wear. Let her go to church without a dress."

He became hard. He was not moved by Gienia's sorrowful letter describing how she prostrated herself in church, begging God's forgiveness for having cheated her beloved uncle, how she kept a candle burning day and night before Błażej's photograph. Błażej scoffed at all that. "I won't give them any more," he repeated. "Nothing."

His nephew Stanisław sent a picture showing his broken arm in a sling, as proof of his new misfortune, and wrote:

Dear Uncle,

In the first words of my letter I send you my greetings and the news that a great misfortune has come upon me. I broke my arm in a bad way. Dear Uncle, I was in a hospital for three weeks and it cost a lot. I have enough troubles as it is, and to have this misfortune on top of others is more than a man can bear. So I write you once more, Dear Uncle, and beg your help, because if you do not come to my help I might as well die, because when one is healthy one can bear many things and oppressions, as I did, but now I'm nothing but a beggar. I can't even chop wood to start the fire to cook food for my children, but must ask people to help me . . . I beg you as best I can . . . I'm enclosing a picture of myself with a broken arm.

Błażej told Wieniawski to write back as follows:

Dear Stanisław,
        You can kiss my ass. You won't swindle me any more.
                        Your uncle,

                    Błażej

P.S. I got your picture with the broken arm.

Wieniawski was surprised that Błażej had become so hardhearted, so set against them. But then, he thought, maybe he doesn't have any money, maybe he is saving it for that holiday trip to Pittsburgh.

"I sent some to Konstanty," he said. "And that's it."

|||

Błażej returned from Pittsburgh in a good mood. He had caught a slight cold there. He was tired, but there was a glow about him. And the same glow shone on Broad Street, clean now and white with fresh snow, sparkling with Christmas decorations. The loudspeakers blared "Jingle Bells" and then, in turn, "Bóg się rodzi," "Wsród nocnej ciszy," and "Silent Night," "Przybieżeli do Betlejem," "O Come All Ye Faithful," and "Lulajże Jezuniu." Near the food market there rose a tall Christmas tree, and Broad Street became festive and gay and full of color, as did Błażej himself. It was obvious that something strange was happening to him, something joyous, and that he had come to some fateful decision, but he didn't know yet how to carry it through. It took a long while before he made up his mind to confide in Wieniawski. He waited patiently one day until the last client had left the office. Then he asked ingratiatingly:

"Want me to bring you some coffee?"

"If you would be so kind, Mr. Twardowski. But it'll be on me today."

Błażej came back slowly, picking his way carefully on the slippery sidewalk. He sat down on his chair across the desk from Wieniawski, took out a cigar, and lit it.

"That Frances," he said. "I bought her a coat."

"You did? How about a new coat for yourself? Look at that rag you're wearing."

Twardowski paid no attention.

"I said to her: 'What do you want for Christmas?' And she said she wanted a coat. So I went with her to the store and told her: 'Pick what you want.' And she picked one for fifty dollars. And I told her: 'That's too cheap, you'd better take one over there, for two hundred dollars.' And she said: 'Now, where would cousin—that's me—get enough money for that coat.' And I said, 'Never mind, that's not your business, there's more where this came from.' She has a fine little boy. He doesn't speak Polish, but wants to learn. He says he wants to go to college."

"Good," said Wieniawski. "Now you have a family of your own."

He thought: "Now perhaps he'll stop pestering me." But he was a little upset, too, because he knew he would miss Błażej. "So when are you moving to Pittsburgh?"

"Moving?" Błażej was surprised at the idea. "No, they have no room for me there. Why should I be a bother to them? I'll go there again some time."

"I thought maybe you'd make your home with them."

"I am old. She has her husband, her children to take care of."

"And if you get sick, who'll take care of you here? No one will ever come to see you in that infernal hole you live in."

"Well, if I get sick, I'll die, that's all there is to it. No need for her to bother with me. But I came here to ask you about that testament."

"Testament?"

Twardowski gave him no chance to ponder. He spoke rapidly, urgently. The light of day died on Broad Street. Street lamps preened in their store window reflections and the multicolored lights on the Christmas tree painted the snow in red and green patches. A light snow began to fall, bringing with it the silence of the sky, muffling all noise.

"I have some money in bonds, and a bit in the bank . . . ."

"So buy yourself a decent coat!"

Twardowski paid no attention.

"All in all, I guess, it'll be around thirty-five thousand."

"Good god!" exclaimed Wieniawski. "That's a fortune! How did you ever manage to save all that? From your weekly paycheck at the steel mill?"

"Used to play horses," Błażej confided. "I was lucky. Saved some from my weekly checks, too. Now you told me—and I asked around, some others say it, too—that if I leave no will, the state will grab all my money."

"You should see a lawyer about this. Mr. Dekrocki can prepare a will for you."

"Ehhh . . . I'd rather you did it . . . ."

"What?"

"I'd rather you looked after things for me."

"You want me to be the executor of your will?"

"That's it. That's it."

"But you have many friends here. Even that cousin from Pittsburgh."

"Yes, but I want everything to be the way I want it, just exactly like I want it."

"Come on, you'll outlive me yet."

"Not me. This is my last year."

"But why do you want me to do it? Such a responsibility!"

Błażej said nothing.

"Why me? You don't really know me at all."

"That's how I want it. Maybe I don't know you, and then maybe I do. I thought to myself, you are the one guy who won't swindle me."

"Antek, listen—" Wieniawski called to Dekrocki, "Błażej Twardowski here wants to make a will."

"Okay, send him in, send him right in." Dekrocki rubbed his hands As usual, a good dinner in a restaurant, a weakness he could not overcome despite occasional and futile efforts to lose weight, had put him in a cheerful mood.

Attorney Dekrocki had both feet firmly planted on the ground: one Polish foot, one American foot. There was no point in tagging him red-and-white or star-spangled, for symbols meant nothing to him. He simply lived. He liked his morning coffee, a piece of toast with a slice of ham (made in Poland), rare steaks, and well-buttered buns. He used salt sparingly and had never eaten anything bitter in his life.

"Isn't this a better way to live?" thought Wieniawski. He liked Dekrocki, even though they often argued heatedly about the salt and the bitterness, which Dekrocki refused even to taste but which spiced Wieniawski's life. Dekrocki was born here and raised here, and it was from here that he took off, as from a springboard, up and away from the immigrant ethnic group he came from. His parents had given him a good education and passed on to him a vague feeling of love for the misty old country.

During his army days, he had met some Poles who immediately had wanted to make him over after their own fashion. They had become his friends, but failed to change him in any way. His respect for his parents and his friendship for his old army buddies brought him closer to Wieniawski and helped him bear with equanimity his partner's tart tongue and his endless Polish tirades.

"Send him right in," mocked Wieniawski. "Business, business, nothing but business!"

"Jasiu, you're crazy."

"I'm crazy and you're greedy. Business and more business! You don't even want to know why Twardowski wants to have a will made."

"I know nothing about him."

"You mean you don't know *him*."

"Okay, I don't know him."

"Why don't you? You never see anything but the end of your own nose. You make your living thanks to these people. You should have a little interest in them."

"Get off my back, will you?"

"I'm just warning you that this man trusts us and we must give him honest advice."

"Jasiu, I'm a lawyer!"

"Lawyer!" muttered Wieniawski. He was angry.

Błażej, on the other hand, felt happy. He rejoiced in the thought that he had found, or rather met, Frances. It was as if he had been groping in the dark and suddenly clasped a friendly hand. From then on, nothing else mattered— not the face, not the appearance of the form—only that outstretched, friendly hand.

"She'll get it all after my death," he thought, and made up his mind to leave everything to Frances.

Wieniawski was present when Błażej's will was drawn up. He was surprised.

"Nothing for your family in the old country?"

"Those vooltures?" bristled Błażej. "The ones who cheated me? I won't give them anything. Nothing."

He grew excited and started pacing the floor, leaning forward, his coat unbuttoned and showing a torn sweater underneath. He muttered to himself angrily, puffing on his cigar, finally throwing it on the parquet floor— something he had never done before—stamping on it and kicking it furiously. He trembled with rage. What was it that had upset him so: his hatred of those "vooltures" or the overwhelming feeling of gratitude toward Frances? Which was more important—the land he had lost, or the memories he had found?

"But they are so miserable," said Wieniawski.

Błażej became even angrier at that. He cursed so loudly that it was as if he wanted to shout himself down.

"Let them drop dead. Damn their thieving eyes! You think they want me? They want my dollars, that's what they want."

"That's true," Wieniawski said some days later. "All they wanted was his money. Still, they are such miserable wretches."

"You're crazy," laughed Dekrocki. "You carry on as if we didn't have trouble enough with money transfers abroad. This way everything will stay here."

"Let me tell you something, Antek. . . ." For some reason Wieniawski felt offended. "You're every bit as much of a vulture as they are. That man isn't dying yet, and here you go already."

Sitting at his desk later, he found it difficult to collect his thoughts. "Why did I get mixed up in all this? Why did I agree to be the executor of his will? Well, I'll get some money. The executor gets a percentage. Damn it, I don't like to profit by someone's death. But he'll outlive me, no doubt. He will." He was calming down little by little, but a feeling of discontent, like a bad aftertaste, stayed with him. "Damn business," he muttered.

"We'll have to deposit his will in court," Dekrocki said, "And he can keep the receipt."

|||

It was in early spring that Błażej's health began to fail. Yes, it was spring—the end of February, or perhaps March. The bay grew lively. A ship from the old country arrived, and the sailors sold their bottles of vodka at the restaurant in the Polish Home. Seagulls swarmed over the square in front of the food market. They snatched stepped-on bits of refuse and flew up, but not very high. Heavy and fat, they alighted on the metal roof of the market. Perhaps it was not only spring that made Błażej ill, but also his second visit to Frances, when he presented her with the gift of the receipt for his last will. Whatever it was, anyway, the old man had lived through three quarters of a century, and his many years hung heavy on his broad shoulders like an old roof on a house that barely hugs the ground with its rotten sills.

Błażej came back from his visit to Pittsburgh out of sorts. "I'll be changing my will," he told Wieniawski.

"What's this all about?"

It took a long while before he told Wieniawski the truth.

"Did they receive you poorly?"

"That's not it. Of course, it wasn't like the first time I was there, when I made her all those promises."

"Well, then, what happened?"

"I told her: 'When you get the money, give it to your boy so he can go to college. Let him be an engineer or a doctor.'"

"What did she say to that?"

"She said, 'I had it tough, why should he have it easier? I'll be damned if I give him any money, it'll just go to his head.'"

"Maybe when you go there again . . . ."

"I won't go. I don't feel good. I can't eat. I've got this thing in my chest, so heavy I can't catch my breath or lie down in peace."

"Yet you won't spend a penny to have a doctor look at you."

"I went to see that guy who has a store on the corner."

"He's not a doctor, he's a druggist."

"He's better than many a doctor. He says he'll give me a medicine only the rich can buy."

"What am I going to do with you?" Wieniawski exclaimed, exasperated.

And as he was wont to do when he was upset and angry, he started berating the inhabitants of Broad Street.

"There's no way to deal with your stupidity! You won't spend a penny for a doctor, you don't trust anyone, you squirrel away under your beds every dollar you have, you go to a drugstore to get some pills, and that's the end of it! But what's needed in your case here is a specialist. Your pills won't help what ails you."

"I'll die anyway. This year is my last."

"Damnation! So kill yourself if you want to. There is no medication for stubbornness. But if you want my advice . . . ."

Before he could go on, a new client entered the office and interrupted him. She was a tiny woman, very shy. A big, plaid gray kerchief tightly covered her forehead and fell over her shoulders, crossed in front, the way old peasant women used to wear them. She minced her steps, embarrassed at finding herself in the office, at being in that strange, vast place.

"Hello, Mrs. Krupczak." Wieniawski greeted her.

Reassured by that recognition, she smiled, showing pale gums, and pushed her kerchief back from her forehead with a motion slightly more bold.

"You remember me. Fancy that! Sweet Jesus!"

She perched carefully on the edge of a chair, like a starved sparrow, frightened half to death, swept into some unknown regions, trembling and overcome by its own daring.

"Yes, I do remember you," said Wieniawski, "You are the lady who sends medications to the old country and keeps it a secret from her children."

"If they ever find out . . . God forbid. They wouldn't let me. But it's my own money."

"What can I do for you?"

"Mr. Wieniawski," she whispered, "What kind of a sickness would that be when one needs two hundred penicillin shots?"

Wieniawski shrugged, "Either they want to open a pharmacy, or they have one already."

Mrs. Krupczak did not detect the sarcasm in Wieniawski's voice.

"Dear, sweet Jesus! And what kind of a sickness would a pharmacy be?" And then, quickly, breathlessly, in a murmur hardly audible from shock: "How much should I send to save them?"

"Ten injections will be enough for now," said Wieniawski. He thought, "Błażej is right. They are 'vooltures.' This is really shocking. How is it that until now I have always felt sorry for them? Whose side am I on?"

Błażej left, somewhat disappointed that he couldn't talk to his heart's content and complain all he wanted. He shuffled along Broad Street aimlessly, a glance here, a brief stop there. All the stores were getting ready for Easter. People were buying new clothes for the Easter parade. The marketplace was teeming. There was a flower stand there, all white and yellow and lilac, with cattails soaking in pails of water.

"Who would ever spend his money for flowers like that?" Błażej wondered.

And on the sidewalk, right by the market, there was a carpet of tulips, hyacinths, and hydrangeas. All Broad Street was abloom. It bloomed, but indifferently, taking no notice of Błażej any more. He was sad and upset. He was disappointed in Frances. He felt ill, very ill and weak. Once again, he thought of his last will. Perhaps he should change it. But there was not enough energy left in him. There was no more talk with Wieniawski about it, though there were many opportunities to do so. When Wieniawski asked:

"Any word from Pittsburgh? No invitation for the holidays?" Błażej only shook his head.

"I wouldn't go there, anyway. Good riddance." He dismissed it with a wave of his hand, then pulled a letter from his coat pocket. "From Gienia. Read it to me."

"You're not angry with Gienia any more?"

"I only want to know what drivel she writes this time."

Wieniawski read:

Dear Uncle,

It's me, Gienia, who dares to write you these few words. You're angry with me, I can't help that, I just want to know whether you are alive and well and if you got that picture of Our Lady I sent you, because I want to know, because this was the dearest thing I had and you haven't deigned to write whether you got it or not. I'll explain right away about this picture. This year, and last year, there was a pilgrimage to Our Lady's shrine in Częstochowa, to pray to Her because a disaster is coming, and so there were many people coming from America, too, and people from our village would go to Warsaw to meet their relatives from America there, and some girls from our village were in Częstochowa when those people from America were there and they told us how they prayed and knelt to kiss their native land, and even took some with them in little bags, so our priest announced at Mass that if anyone had a relative abroad, he should recommend him to the good graces of Our Lady of Częstochowa on that day and get a picture of Her and send it off to him, and it would be as if that relative had visited Częstochowa himself on a pilgrimage. So there were some people from our village who went to Częstochowa, and I asked them to bring me back a picture of Our Lady so I could send it to my beloved uncle, so that Our Lady would watch over him, because he has no one to take care of him, but you haven't deigned to write if you received it or not, and I am worried that perhaps it did not get there and perished on its way. It is too bad you are angry with me, but I don't know how to lie the way Konstanty does. It was Konstanty who said you had no right to that land after all these years in America, and now that you are sending him all that money at least his son has something to drink away. They say it's like a new lease on life when they get those American dollars. They don't want to work, because they don't have to, and they are healthy. The son married a girl who brought him some land in her dowry, but he does not want to work, only looks for handouts, won't bother with stock but keeps only one cow and one horse so he won't have to pay taxes, and if the tax man comes around, there's nothing he can take and so he goes away, because they don't want to work . . . .

"She writes nothing about money?" asked Błażej.

"No."

"Good. Write her I'm sick and will have to go to the hospital."

Wieniawski put down the letter and looked at Błażej. The old man did not look well at all. He had aged visibly and diminished in strength. He seemed so old and lonely in his illness, so unwanted that, without stopping to think it over, Wieniawski said:

"If you have no plans for the holiday, why don't you come to our house? There'll be a few people, you'll have someone to talk to."

Błażej's face lit up.

"I have a good suit," he assured Wieniawski, as if he wanted to say: "Have no fear, I won't embarrass you."

He behaved solemnly and with dignity when he entered among Wieniawski's books and paintings, when he sat down at the holiday table gleaming with white linen. Then later, seated comfortably on a soft armchair, within the pink circle of the drawing room lamp, he chatted with other guests. It was only at the end of the evening that he began to feel weak and asked to be taken home.

"Look at that," he mused. "He invited me home, and Frances didn't . . . A stranger took me into his home and that one, the one I gave everything I had, didn't. Why?"

That summer was difficult for Błażej. It seemed hotter and more humid than usual. When he walked along Broad Street, he didn't so much walk as struggle with every step he made; he didn't move along the sidewalk, but pushed his way through sticky screens of heat. Sometimes it seemed to him that he was back in the steel mill; the hot, heavy sheets of steel taxed his strength, blocked his way, lay heavy on his chest, took his breath away. He could not sleep. In fitful dreams, he heard the roar of the furnaces and sweated in the clouds of steam given off by hot metal, filling his nostrils and his ears. Or he felt as if someone had put a huge clock in his chest. It ticked fast at first, and then slower and stronger, till it became a grandfather clock whose mighty pendulum struck against his rib cage, as if meaning to break it. He would wake from those half-naps, half-swoons, drenched with sweat, worn out, only to be caught up again in the cobwebs of nightmares sealing his eyes and his mouth. He would awake with an attack of asthma, shivering with chills, then cover himself up to the chin with a blanket and wait, curled up and trembling, for the arrival of the day. When the first rosy light of the morning looked in on him and then, changing to blue, alighted on his sinewy, trembling hands, Błażej would drag himself from his cot and, looking at the roofs of houses along St. Agnes Street, at the silver waterfall of sunlight, he would say to himself:

"One more day."

He could not eat much. Chicken broth tasted foul, and his throat refused to swallow bread. What he liked best was to sit in Wieniawski's office, where two strong fans made the heat a little more bearable, to sip his coffee and smoke his cigar, saying little or nothing at all.

"You should go to the seashore," Wieniawski told him. "It's cooler there, there's a breeze. We'll find you a nice boarding house."

"That's not for me," Błażej shrugged. "I wouldn't last through the trip."

He watched avidly the goings-on of Broad Street: the traffic, the house-wives walking to the food market and coming back with their bags full of groceries. In the afternoon, he would take his chair outside and sit on the sidewalk in front of the office, just looking. From where he sat he could see the street well, as it climbed steeply and disappeared somewhere on the red, hot horizon, like a hissing branding iron dipped in ice-cold water. On the right, the big hospital dome rose like a huge green onion. There were no trees on Broad Street. Only the sky, the air, and the smells coming from the bay marked the passing of seasons. Not a leaf there, not a flower, not even a wilted one, withered with heat.

Sometimes when Wieniawski had to go out he would leave the office in Twardowski's care. At such times the old man would place himself near the doorway, watch it carefully, and, conscious of the importance of his task, inform all clients at what time Wieniawski would return.

"You don't look well," fretted Wieniawski. "You really should go and see a doctor."

But Błażej would not listen to him.

"Once the summer's over, I'll be all right. It's the heat that's bothering me."

One day, in the beginning of October, when the sun was still hot, Błażej stopped at the Albatross office as usual, just before noon. Attorney Dekrocki, just back from his vacation, was discussing with Wieniawski the case he was to defend in court the following day, in which Wieniawski was to act as official interpreter.

"What kind of a lawyer are you?" Wieniawski shouted. "You have a case in court tomorrow and nothing's ready yet."

"Jasiu, don't be crazy. I am a lawyer and I assure you I have all the time I need."

"You always think there's plenty of time. What do you care if they deport that man . . . ."

"The pittance he paid me . . . ."

"There you go again."

"Jasiu, you're crazy."

"You sit down at your desk right this minute. Where do you have those papers? Where do you keep them? God Almighty, what a mess you are! How can you work like this?"

"Mr. Wieniawski, " Błażej put in.

"Just a moment, Mr. Twardowski. Just one moment. You can see for yourself what's going on here. I can't read your letters now. Perhaps tomorrow . . . ."

Błażej did not answer. He leaned against the wall. He was tired. "Why did I come here?" he thought. He could not remember what it was he wanted to ask Wieniawski about.

A letter? That's right. He had a letter in his pocket. The last will . . . was that it? Or had he just wanted to get some coffee? That was it—he'd go bring some coffee. He tried to take a few steps, to detach himself from the wall. Strangely, the wall would not let him go, but followed him, crashed on top of his chest, and choked his breath out.

"So heavy . . . ," he moaned, and fell to the parquet floor.

Dekrocki and Wieniawski rushed to him.

"What happened? What is it? Błażej! Błażej! Antek, call an ambulance. Hurry!"

"Błażej . . . ." Wieniawski tugged at his sleeve. From the pocket of the old man's greasy, worn coat a blue envelope fluttered to the floor.

Alerted by Dekrocki, two of Błażej's buddies and the barman came running from the Polish Home. Together they lifted Błażej and tried to revive him with water. But the old man was unconscious. He breathed in quick, faint, shallow gasps.

The siren of the ambulance could be heard down the length of Broad Street. A group of men left the bar at the Polish Home and stood outside. A few curious passersby stopped at the door of the Albatross.

"Twardowski?" they said. "Is that Twardowski? What happened to him? He was walking by only now. We just saw him."

They put Błażej on a stretcher. "Is there anyone from his family here?" asked the attendant.

And then everyone—Dekrocki, the barman, Błażej's cronies, the men from the Polish Home—everyone looked at Jan Wieniawski.

"I'll be right back," he said and he left the office, following the stretcher with the unconscious old man.

When Błażej woke up, he felt an iron hoop tight around his chest. He was nauseated. He felt a pain in his right hand. He looked around him and saw he was half covered with a veil-like plastic sheet. A rubber tube attached to a downward-tilted bottle was connected to his wrist, feeding drop after drop into the vein. Błażej closed his eyes, then opened them again and looked around. He was in a small rectangular room. In the next bed, a man lay curled up and moaning. On the other side of the room, another man, half reclining in bed, was eating bread and sausage, apparently brought in by the woman sitting at his side.

"Water . . . ," moaned Błażej.

No one heard him.

He thought, "I'm not dead yet. I'm still alive." He moved slightly, but immediately felt such a piercing pain in his chest that he gave a loud, long moan. The man on the other side of the room heard him this time.

"Press the bell!" he called out.

"What's he saying?" thought Błażej as he slipped into numbness. When he came to, he saw Wieniawski at the foot of his bed. He could not talk, but he stretched out both his trembling hands from under the oxygen tent and tried to smile.

"Błażej," said Wieniawski. "Do you recognize me?"

The old man nodded.

"I sent a telegram to Frances, telling her to come."

Błażej tried to smile, to say something, but he could not. Only his eyes, gray, weary, and sunken, seeming somehow larger and moist, could speak.

"Would you like something to drink?"

He nodded. Wieniawski poured a glass of water, put in a bent straw, and brought it to Błażej's lips.

"I sent a telegram to Frances . . . ," he began again. But Błażej closed his eyes, turned his head away, and, it seemed, fell asleep.

Wieniawski went out into the corridor, looked for the doctor's room, and went in.

"What is the condition of Błażej Twardowski?" he said.

The doctor on duty looked up from the big book in which he was writing. "Yes?"

"I'm asking about the condition of Błażej Twardowski. He was brought here yesterday afternoon."

A nurse passing by saw Wieniawski.

"You can't go in there," she called out to him. "This is the doctors' room."

"My dear lady," said Wieniawski. "Mind your own business."

The doctor winked at her, and the nurse left.

"Are you a relative of his?" the doctor asked.

"No, but I'm taking care of him. I took care of all the red tape, the hospital called me about him. Everything was in order as long as I could get some money. But when one needs something from you . . . ."

"Just a moment. I'll check. But, you understand, our rules . . . ."

"My dear doctor, I don't have time for your rules and regulations. You think you're gods, you build yourselves a fortress of regulations, and then you take money from men's pockets according to those regulations. I want to know what is the matter with that patient?"

"You don't like us," smiled the doctor. He was a burly young man with curly hair. "Just a moment, just a moment, let me see. How do you spell that name? Here it is. Cancer of both lungs. Advanced case. Badly neglected. They operated yesterday and drained the fluid."

"Will he . . . ?"

"The prognosis is not good. I can't tell you any more. I'm not his doctor. I'm on duty here now. I think it would be best if someone from his family came."

On his way back, Wieniawski lost his way and wandered through the complex of hospital corridors for a long time. "What a colossus!" he thought. "What a tremendous power! Now then, is that the way I came? To the left here, or to the right?" Loudspeakers mounted at several points called out doctors' names; "Doctor Coleman! Doctor Sneider! Doctor Russell Sneider!"

Wieniawski hesitated. He stopped. Everything here seemed the same: dozens of doors, floors and mezzanines, corridors, passages, stairways, elevators, all crowded with bustling, jostling people in a hurry: blacks, whites, and Asians, people in street clothes, nurses in their starched white uniforms, small knots of physicians talking in low voices, a nurse from the operating room with a gauze mask half hiding her face, patients in wheelchairs, patients on stretchers, conscious and semiconscious. Wieniawski moved to one side because they were bringing in a patient with two rubber tubes protruding from his nostrils. An orderly pushed the gurney, and a nurse was walking alongside, holding the bottle connected to the tubes.

"Doctor Burton . . . Doctor Harry Burton," called the loudspeaker. And then: "Doctor Wilkinson . . . Doctor David Wilkinson!"

Another gurney passed by carrying a small boy. The child, a boy perhaps seven years old, had a paper-white face, an elongated skull with a hideous bump on the forehead, and such infinite sadness, such lonely childish suffering in his eyes and in the twist of his mouth that Wieniawski, filled with horror and yet with respect and sympathy, moved quickly aside only to bump into a young man who had but one-fourth of a face. His cheeks formed hideous, scarred-over pits, his eyes and nose ran in a slanted line across a face that retained, still, the remains of human expression. Wieniawski stopped one of the orderlies.

"Where's the exit?"

"Where do you want to go?"

"Broad Street."

Again he wandered, brushing against stretchers and gurneys, making his way amid timid groans subdued by sedatives.

"They say there is a world of the living and a world of the dead," he thought. "But that's not true. There is also a third world, a world of the sick and the suffering, a huge world, clammy like the body of a monstrous jellyfish, slimy and foggy, difficult to escape. The torture of non-life and non-death. Run, run, run away from here!" But the hospital corridors pressed in on him from all sides, pulled him back, and locked him in. It took Wieniawski a long time to find his way to the Broad Street exit. Along his way he passed the hospital cafeteria, then the small post office, a branch office of a bank. He lost his way again and again, and finally emerged in the main lobby of the hospital, dominated by an oversize statue of Christ. This part of the lobby was poorly lighted, and the statue's head was lost in the shadows drifting down from the ceiling. Only Christ's outstretched hands and powerful feet of gray stone could be seen clearly.

"It's a city, not a hospital," muttered Wieniawski. "I lost so much time. Well, anyway, today or tomorrow Frances will come and take care of Błażej."

But Frances did not come until three days later. She arrived with her husband, and they first went to the Albatross office. She was an elderly woman, quiet in manner, dressed in city clothes and a flowered hat.

"How is my cousin?" she asked in English.

"I should be asking you that question!" Wieniawski exploded. He was angry with Frances for coming so late.

"I couldn't come any sooner," she explained. "But we'll go visit him right away."

Frances's husband sat to one side and looked over the office. He wore glasses and had full but flabby cheeks. He complained that the trip had been tiresome and that he was hungry. They left for the hospital but returned so promptly that Wieniawski was amazed.

"Back already?" he asked.

"Sure," said Frances. "There is no emergency of any kind. He's not dying yet."

"Where are you going to stay? I have the keys to his apartment."

"We're going home right away," she answered. "If anything happens . . . you understand . . . please give us a call."

"What do you mean?" shouted Wieniawski, "You won't stay here with him? You're going to leave him alone just like that?"

"Mr. Wieniawski, I have a house, a husband, and children to take care of."

"But how can you? That man has left you his entire estate, he is sick, he has no family here, and you're about to take off? You came to see him just once after he waited all that time? . . . He gave you everything he had, his life's blood, and now you . . . ."

Frances looked with surprise at Wieniawski's red face. She repeated: "If anything happens . . . ."

"Where can I get a beer around here?" asked her husband. Wieniawski directed them to the Polish Home and said no more. After office hours, tired and furious, he went to see Błażej.

The old man was lying with his eyes open. Again, as before, he stretched out both arms to Wieniawski.

"It's good you came . . . ," he said. His voice sounded changed. His dentures, wrapped in a piece of gauze, were soaking in a glass of water on the night table.

Wieniawski also was glad to see Błażej.

"See, Błażej, see how much better you are today."

"I'd like to see a priest. I want to confess."

"All right, I'll call him. I'll talk to the doctor, too. I'll tell him to spare no expense to get you well. And I'll tell your buddies over at the Polish Home to come and see you."

"Frances was here," Błażej confided. "She did come."

"I know, I know. She was at the office, too."

As he was leaving, Błażej tried to raise himself on the bed.

Again stretching both his arms from under the oxygen tent he whispered: "Thank you, thank you . . . ."

That was how he greeted and thanked Wieniawski every night, stretching out both arms as if he wanted to embrace him, for it was every night, after office hours, that Wieniawski came to the hospital to see Błażej. There was no sign of life from Frances. The buddies from the Polish Home came once or twice and then no more. Only Wieniawski—vowing every night that this was the last time, that he'd let a few days go before coming again, that he had no time, damn it—only Wieniawski returned to the hospital each day. Just as Błażej in days past had walked each day along Broad Street to the Albatross, so now Wieniawski, after closing the travel office, drove or walked each day up Broad Street, past the marketplace and on to the hospital to visit Błażej. It would be difficult to explain why he did it. People are forever either paying a debt or contracting one, without ever knowing whom they are paying back or from whom they are borrowing.

One evening in November, when Błażej lay in his bed, weak but fully conscious, Wieniawski brought him a letter from his nephew Stanisław. Twardowski's former roommates had long since gone home, and new patients moaned in their beds. Only Błażej had not left his place under the oxygen tent.

"How goes it?" asked Wieniawski.

"I can't eat anything," complained Błażej, "And that nurse won't even look in on me."

Wieniawski hurried to the nurses' station immediately and demanded better care for Błażej.

"When a man is so down and out he can't even call for help, you're content to leave him to God's mercy, and yet you're quick enough when it comes to collecting money," he stormed.

"I told them," he reassured Błażej. "The nurse will feed you, Błażej, she'll give you an injection if you need one."

"Thank you."

Błażej said "thank you" often now, though he never used to much before.

"Stanisław writes . . . ."

"Please, read it to me," asked Błażej.

Wieniawski read:

Dear Uncle,
   In the first words of my letter I send you my greetings and ask about your health. Dear Uncle, I keep praying to God and asking Him for good health for you, and since you helped me out of my trouble I could finish the barn, but now I have another trouble, I had no milk for the children, so I got a loan from the milk cooperative to buy a cow and I bought my children a cow and now I have a heifer from that cow and would not like to sell it, but the government debt is heavy on me and I have to do something, so I'm sending you, Dear Uncle, the paper I got from them.

Wieniawski took out of the envelope a flimsy scrap of paper, a message from the Cooperative Bank, "calling on Citizen to pay immediately the interest due for one year, amounting to two hundred sixty-nine zlotys and sixty-four groszy for the cow acquired on credit."

Błażej made a wry face.

"Nothing but money," he sighed. "Only money."

He was silent for a long while. Wieniawski thought he had fallen asleep. He put the letter on the night table by the bedside and was about to leave, when Twardowski stretched out his hand.

"What is it?" leaned over Wieniawski.

"Is that all he writes?"

Wieniawski could not decide whether the old man really wanted to know what was in the letter, or whether he merely wanted to keep him from leaving.

"There is some more. But I thought you were asleep."

"Please, read."

"I learned that you are not well, Dear Uncle . . . ," wrote Stanisław.

"He must have learned that from earlier letters. He couldn't have heard about the hospital yet," interrupted Wieniawski.

"Well?" Błażej prompted.

. . . and that you left all your life's work, your whole American estate, to Bogula's daughter, which is fine, as you have done it already and it can't be undone, but if you had it in mind, Dear Uncle, to send me some money, I would have Gregorian Masses said for your soul, after your death, as I had done for the souls of Józefa and Stefan, my mother and father, I would have a funeral Mass said and would put up a tombstone like our priest had done for another priest. You asked me once about that priest, Father Jan Lipa, who always used to ask about you . . . .

Błażej started and tried to sit up in bed, but failed.

"Jasiek Lipa?" he whispered in a voice so changed, so muffled that Wieniawski did not hear it and went on reading.

. . . the Soviets deported him and his whole family to Siberia, and they all, and Father Lipa, too, died there, and our priest here put up a tombstone and it says on it where they died and that all who pass by are asked to say one Hail Mary. And I could also have a porcelain picture of you made up to put on the tombstone, because I have five photographs of you. Dear Uncle, please keep it in mind that I could have a tombstone made for you just like the one for my parents and if you want me to I'll send you a picture of it. Dear Uncle, things do not go well for me . . . .

"What is it, Błażej?" Twardowski beckoned for him to lean closer. Wieniawski put his ear close to the old man's cracked, parched lips.

"Jasiek died?"

Wieniawski nodded.

"He's not buried in the village?"

"Only his tombstone is there."

"They took him to Siberia and he died there?"

"That's what he writes."

Błażej closed his eyes, did not say another word, turned his face to the wall. Wieniawski waited a while yet, then he left. He stopped at the hospital office to fill out more forms. The four weeks Błażej had stayed at the hospital had cost well over a thousand dollars already.

"After thirty days, his insurance payments will stop," thought Wieniawski. "They notified me already. And if he has to stay much longer, all his savings will be gone, most of his life savings will go for doctors, nurses, and medications. Is that what he slaved for all his life? Is that what he was skimping and saving for? That Jasiek Lipa . . . the one he kept asking about. He's dead."

But then the bustle of the hospital and of Broad Street claimed Wieniawski. "Well, I stayed with him a good long while," he thought. "Now I can finally go home, read the paper, and watch some TV."

His face turned toward the green hospital wall, Błażej was thinking about Jasiek Lipa.

Every night Błażej asked Wieniawski whether there was anything from Frances. A letter? A phone call? But there was neither. Instead, letters from the old country poured in. Wieniawski brought them to the hospital and, because he could not talk much with Błażej anyway, he read them to him. Błażej listened, more or less indifferently.

"Dear Uncle," wrote Gienia,

> My dearest father, for you are truly like a father to me, and now you have this sadness and pain happen to you, we are much aggrieved. I went to our priest immediately and gave him an offering to say a Holy Mass for your health . . . .

There was also a letter from Stanisław:

Yesterday I learned from the letter that you are seriously ill and in your illness you are remembering all Poles and us, your family. Yesterday we all here prayed for your recovery, and I showed the children your picture and told them to pray for you, because you are very sick, and I went to see the priest today and gave him an offering to say a Mass for you. To end these few words, I ask that you write us, we are waiting with impatience, we wish you good health.

Your nephew,
Stanisław and family

Józek, the third child of Błażej's late sister, also wrote:

Dear Uncle,
We all know we must die some time. When?—only God knows. Do not worry that you have no family to remember your soul, because I will never forget about your soul. Even today I took an offering to our priest and asked him to say a Mass for your prompt recovery. The Mass was celebrated on November 10, at seven o'clock (Polish time).

Thanksgiving Day came. Błażej was lonely in the hospital. He waited for Frances. He was almost sure she'd come. Over the long years in America he had come to understand and value the feast of Thanksgiving. It was somewhat like Christmas Eve in the old country—families gathered at the table, and no one went forgotten or lonely.

"She'll come," he kept telling himself joyously. "She'll come."

None of his old buddies visited him any more. Even Wieniawski had announced that he would not be coming to see him on Thanksgiving. Błażej did not know himself why he wanted so much to see Frances on that particular day, why he awaited her coming so eagerly. Was it to reassure himself that he, too, had a family here in America?

"She should come," he reasoned. "I left everything to her."

The hours passed slowly. The nurse went through the wards with dinner trays on a cart, then she brought in the evening medication. Daylight faded outside the window.

"Now she'll come," thought Błażej. He heard a click of heels in the corridor and tried to raise himself on his elbows. But these were not his guests. They went to see someone else.

"It's Thanksgiving today. She'll come," he reassured himself. "Any time now, she'll be here."

He concentrated on the door of the room, left slightly ajar, but then a new wave of pain gripped him, he couldn't breathe, and he vomited. Exhausted, he closed his eyes. He felt a light touch on his arm. Frances? No, it was the nurse to take his temperature. She asked why he hadn't eaten his dinner.

He smiled bitterly. How could he eat? He could not raise himself and neither dared to nor knew how to ask for someone to feed him. He fell asleep. It was past midnight when he woke up. A small night light was on at the far end of the room. The new patient had just had an operation, and a private nurse was sitting by his bedside. Silence. Błażej realized that Thanksgiving Day was over and Frances had not come.

"I gave her everything," he sighed. "All my savings."

He had saved all his life. He remembered how every week, year after year, he had gone to the bank to add to his savings book or to buy some bonds. How much did I save this week? How much will I have next week? How much does it come to now? How much will the bank add in interest? It was as if he had been saving himself, taking himself to a safe place, accumulating, giving nothing of himself to others. And when the time came that he wanted to give it all away, to offer it to someone, his money was welcomed, but not Błażej himself. He groaned. No one heard him. He ached all over, and his lips were dry. He had had nothing to drink since morning and could not reach for water. Despite the oxygen tent, he was suffocating.

"I'm dying," he whispered. "I'll die this night."

He moaned again loudly, painfully. He raised his hand and, mustering all his strength, pressed the bell.

He shuddered when someone touched his shoulder. A nurse stood by his side with a syringe.

"I will give you a needle."

Frightened, he looked at the syringe.

"You will sleep better."

A slight prick, a sting in his forearm. For a moment he thought his pain grew bolder, and he groaned again, but then, gradually, a blessed feeling of relief poured through his veins.

He shuddered again. Was someone calling him? Did he really hear someone call his name?

"Błażek! Błaaażek!"

"Right away!" he called back. "Coming!"

He ran out onto the road. The sun was hot, and he had to shade his eyes. The sand of the road burned his bare feet. Jasiek was waiting for him. He squatted near the fence separating the road from the pastures, and with a long stalk of weed was chasing away the flies that buzzed everywhere, stinging the way they always did before a storm.

"It'll rain. It's so hot, and the flies sting so."

They went off together. Jasiek first, Błażek right behind him. He could barely keep up with Jasiek, he was so out of breath. Just beyond the meadow, to the right the woods began, and to the left the wheat inclined its heavy, ripe ears. They stretched out on a strip of grass between two fields. Jasiek took a book out of his pants pocket. He pointed: "Here."

Błażek dangled his legs in the air. A bumblebee alighted on a nearby corn cockle, an obese, plush fellow, so heavy that the weed trembled and bent with his weight. Jasiek moved his finger along the printed lines from word to word, and Błażek's sleepy eyes followed the finger lazily. The bumblebee pulled itself from the flower, buzzed loudly past Błażek's ear, and flew off. Thunder rumbled, so loudly that Błażek felt the earth tremble, and suddenly the first heavy drop of rain fell on Błażek's nose. A storm was coming.

"Don't be afraid." Jasiek got up. He was barefoot, and the back of his shirt was torn. He was looking at Błażek. A sudden gust of wind swept the wheat field into waves. Clouds raced across the sky, fast and low, and bolts of lightning zigzagged after them.

"Jesus," Błażej groaned. He sprang to his feet and began to run.

"Błażek! Błażek! Wait! Look!"

But he would not wait. He ran so fast he couldn't catch his breath. It became dark, the blinding rain thudded steadily, the earth shuddered with each thunder, his feet bogged down in mud.

"Błaaażek! Błaaażek!"

He did not look back. He fled blindly, the road stretching endlessly before him. He couldn't see. He was lost, but kept on running, not caring where, away, away. An ever-fainter voice was calling after him: "Błażek, Błażek." Ever more faint, ever weaker, while the cold rain flogged his face and took his breath away. It was dark. He was lost and wandering. There were no fences, nor fields, nor roads, and the village was nowhere to be seen. Only rain.

"Mr. Wieniawski," said the organist. "You have a call from the hospital."

"Błażej died," breathed Wieniawski, "He died. And I didn't even go to see him yesterday."

"Hello," he said into the receiver. "What happened? When?"

"No, no," the nurse reassured him. "The patient only asked me to tell you to please be sure to come today."

"I'll be right over," Wieniawski said. He turned to Stefański. "I'm going to the hospital. I'm afraid Twardowski has taken a turn for the worse. Would you be so kind and take care of everything here?"

He entered Błażej's room almost at a run. "What is it? What happened?" Błażej was sitting up in bed, for the first time since he had entered the hospital. He stretched out both his arms toward Wieniawski.

"You came," he rejoiced. "You did come. I thought you'd left me for good."

"Are you feeling better?"

"I want to change my last will," Błażej said.

"Right now?"

"It must be today. Call the lawyer."

"Today? Let's wait till after Sunday. What's so urgent? Why such a hurry?"

"I want to change my will, to leave my money to the other ones."

"The other ones? Those in the old country?" Wieniawski was surprised. "But you called them vultures yourself. You said you didn't want to have anything to do with them."

Twardowski smiled.

"Vooltures they are, but they are poor. Poor and dumb," he said gently.

He was tired. He lay back on his pillows and was silent a long time. Wieniawski watched him. In the one day he hadn't seen Błażej, the old man had taken a noticeable turn for the worse. Wieniawski was overcome with pity. Poor Błażej. What torment he was going through, how he kept groping for something in his life.

"What do you think?" asked Błażej. "How much for Gienia?"

"Gienia, too?"

"She has children."

"For Stanisław, and Józek, and Wikta, and Konstanty's son . . . Only one condition," he continued.

"What's that?" asked Wieniawski.

"They must send their children to schools, not drive them to work too early, but educate them to be priests or doctors or teachers. That's my condition. And also . . . ."

He was out of breath again. He started coughing. Wieniawski brought him a glass of water.

"I want to die now. I'll die in peace. I can't eat anyway, and there's no one to help me," he complained.

"Let's hire a private nurse to take care of you. Why should you skimp so now?"

"Too much money. Can't spend all that money. You tell the lawyer to come over today."

"Did you really make up your mind to do it this way? Are you sure?"

He nodded.

"The lawyer will cost money."

"Never mind. Have him come right away. I might not live through the night."

"All right."

"I'd like one more thing. Put up a stone for me. White. With my name and my picture on it. Then take a picture of it and send it to all of them."

"All right. You tell it to the lawyer."

"I don't trust anyone. I don't know what he'll write. You promise me it'll be written up like I want it. And a tombstone with my picture on it."

"I promise."

That evening, at Błażej's bedside, Dekrocki prepared the second will. It was witnessed by a doctor, who confirmed that the patient was of sound mind, and by the man who shared the hospital room with Błażej.

The next day Twardowski grew weaker, and late that evening Wieniawski called the priest.

"You're dying, Błażej," the priest said. "The church needs a new floor. It would be nice if you left something for the church."

It angered Błażej, the way the priest talked. He still had enough strength left to have the personnel man from the steel mill summoned to his bedside and to change the terms of his insurance policy, which had been to go to the church.

"If they're so greedy, they'll get only three hundred dollars," he grumbled, "instead of the three thousand they were going to get. Everything else goes to the estate."

By then no one came to see Błażej any more, except for Wieniawski.

"That president of the Polish Home, he won't even come," Błażej complained. "And I voted for him, too."

He cried from the pain and shortness of breath that tormented him day and night. He complained that he couldn't turn over on his side and that the nurse wouldn't even look in on him. Finally, after much haggling, he consented to Wieniawski's suggestion to call in a private nurse. This happened during the last week of his life. He lay more comfortably, clean-shaven and washed, and a black nurse read the paper to him. Still he grew weaker each day. He was dying.

"It took all that big trouble to get me some service at last," he would say. "She comes in at seven o'clock in the morning, she shaves me—she shaves real good—and washes me off. 'Błażej,' she says, 'how about raising yourself a little.' She reads a while, and when she leaves for the day it feels lonely."

Still, each evening, he argued with Wieniawski, weak as he was, that they should let the nurse go.

"All that money . . . ," he scolded. "Sixteen dollars a day. Better save it for those folks in the old country. They're poor."

His passion for scrimping every penny didn't leave him until the day he died. He had always denied himself, but now, perhaps, he no longer felt sorry for himself.

Christmas was drawing near. The first snow fell, and Broad Street brightened up again. There was a preholiday bustle in the marketplace. The lights of the tall Christmas tree danced red and green on the snow. The loudspeakers blared one Christmas carol after another: "Bóg się rodzi," "Jingle Bells," "Wsród nocnej ciszy," "O Come All Ye Faithful," and "Lulajże Jezuniu." A few frosty stars blinked in the corridor of sky above Broad Street. New snow was in the offing, and slow, gray clouds swept the sky.

It was six o'clock in the evening when the hospital notified Wieniawski that Błażej was dead. Wieniawski started for the hospital, then turned back again. He stopped at a flower shop on St. Agnes Street and bought a large bouquet of long-stemmed white roses.

"He never spent a penny on himself." Wieniawski rationalized the expense, for he was always reluctant to express his real feelings and liked to spend his money carefully and deliberately. "He even let the nurse go a day before he died. I just couldn't argue with him any more about it."

Holding the long flower box under his arm, Wieniawski stopped in front of the hospital gates and looked at Broad Street.

"Something's changed here," he muttered. "The street doesn't look quite so bad anymore. Perhaps it's the snow and all those Christmas baubles. But then, perhaps I'm the one who has changed? Bah! A man doesn't change. Never mind Twardowski and that second will he made . . . ."

Then he went in to see Błażej.

Translated by Marta Erdman

Jocasta

I was walking down a narrow little street in an old town.

It seemed as if the façades of the row houses had bent forward and almost closed overhead in a sort of arch. They formed a vault through which only very little daylight was seeping. I saw her in this twilight, as she came straight toward me in a wheelchair like the one she had used in her last apartment.

I wanted to back away, but she had noticed me already. Her dark and sunken eyes, in a small face no larger than a fist, were fixed on me with an intensity that made me feel rooted to the place. She was wearing a funny little cap on her head, the way she used to in her last, her fourth, apartment. But this was not the white cap of an old lady, more a black beret, tilted over one ear, the way an artist in the Latin Quarter in Paris might wear it.

Instantly—in that illogical way of the world of dreams—she was at my side and she was inviting me for a cup of tea. Her invitation was insistent, and, as I remembered that I had not seen her in a long time, I felt some remorse.

She took me to an antique shop. It did not look like any of her apartments, but the huge antique wardrobe I remembered from her second apartment was there, standing against the wall. The shop was dim, the only light coming from the street through the half-glassed door.

Everything inside was covered with cobwebs and an air of such mystery that we both spoke in a half-whisper, as if this were a rule and a condition for being admitted to this place.

Henryka did not have the slightest intention of serving any tea. Turning her back to me (she was wearing a fetching robe from under which peeped a scanty nightdress), she busied herself in pulling out some large pieces of cardboard stacked against the wall.

In the meantime I was looking at the small pieces of old silver displayed on the counter. The antique sugar bowl, the carved teaspoons, the ashtrays—they all seemed strangely familiar to me.

There was some jewelry arranged in a display case, but I couldn't get a good look at it because Henryka came to me and, lowering her voice even further and looking around suspiciously as if she feared someone would walk in and overhear us, she whispered: "Come here. I would like you to have this." With a vigorous jerk of her strong chin, now even more prominent and determined in her shrunken face, she pointed at the wall.

"This thing." She brought me closer to the wall and pulled out a large sheet of cardboard, frayed at the edges. She turned it toward me, and I saw it was a drawing: overlapping sketches of a woman's profile.

"Take it, take it," she insisted. "Take it before someone walks in here. I would not want this to go to a stranger."

She was also holding another piece of cardboard, but with the drawing turned toward the floor. "And what's this?" I asked.

"Well," she replied, frowning. "You've seen this one before." She laughed with her toothless mouth. "This one goes into the trash." And she flung it into the corner of the antique shop, where it lay on a pile of old papers.

"That was my dream," she explained. "Do you remember?"

"The chasm?"

"Yes," she said. "But now I know better."

I turned to the sketch of the heads to look at them while she hovered at my side, watching closely. She knew I did not want to accept her gift, but she was stubborn, as usual, and determined to have her way. Four profiles of the same woman—it was not difficult to recognize them as profiles of Henryka herself—four different aspects of her face, which traced the history of the last seventeen years of her life.

"Do you like it?" She came closer, but I moved away automatically and realized that she had noticed it.

"A very interesting sketch," I said.

"You don't have to like it," she giggled. "All that matters is that you take it."

"Thank you," I said, but I really felt like tossing it on the pile of old papers in the corner.

Henryka saw my gesture and stopped me. And before I could throw the sketch away, I awoke.

I puzzled over the meaning of that dream. It was the first time I had dreamt of Henryka since her death in October. And here it was, close to the end of January. I would have preferred to forget about her and consider the books closed. She had given me her plants to take care of, and I had gone to her funeral. What more did she want now, asking me to come into the antique shop and offering me the drawing? The truth about herself? She knew full well that it would be harsh. She was older than I by forty years and could have been my grandmother, but she knew the age difference was no barrier to my seeing what she would have preferred to hide.

Henryka arrived in Monumental City in the midfifties. It must have been around 1955, but I did not meet her until a year later. By then she had already left her son's home and was living in her first apartment. In those days, many lonely and widowed women were leaving Poland to join their sons or daughters in the United States. Bitter and disappointed, many of them later went back home, but Henryka stayed. She had severed all her ties when she left Poland. She was going to start a new life here.

A mutual friend who was visiting Monumental City brought Henryka to my house, saying, "I don't know her well myself, but she took care of my mother back in Poland, and that is how I met her. She is very lonely. I think there is some trouble between her and her son—or rather, her daughter-in-law. She doesn't talk about it, though."

Henryka de Chatin was seventy when I met her. She was a big, powerfully built woman with somewhat heavy hips, tall, straight as a ramrod, meticulously and elegantly dressed. She reminded me of a bird of prey, for she had a sharp profile and shiny brown eyes that she sometimes half-veiled by drooping thin, paperlike lids over them. Her strong, muscular arms tinkled with bracelets that fell over her wrists. Her hands were capable and work-worn, with long fingers withered by age and adorned with a wedding band and several antique rings now almost too big for her.

She would not talk about her past or why she had come to America, but the reason for her being in Monumental City was her only son, who had married in Germany and, with his wife and a small son, had emigrated to the United States and settled in Monumental City. All Henryka wanted to talk about was the present and how, or where, she could earn a little money to add to her very modest income.

One could guess she was, in fact, dependent on her son's help and was embarrassed and even tormented by her predicament. She talked about her part-time work in the museum, where her job was to retouch the negatives of the photographs of exhibits. It paid her very little.

As the two ladies were leaving, my friend took me aside and whispered, "She changed her name. She was not de Chatin." I was intrigued and asked why.

"Well, I never really asked. But perhaps her daughter-in-law, or perhaps her son, did not want her to have such a Polish name. Her name used to be Szatkowska. They were expelled from western Poland."

Henryka's first apartment was in that section of downtown where fairly prosperous working families lived in row houses of slightly crumbling red brick. In front of the house there was a small yard with a single rosebush, half-wild and never pruned, but still flowering. I climbed the wooden stairs to the second floor, where a narrow corridor led to the kitchen, a bathroom, and a largish room that served as Henryka's bedroom and sitting room.

"Sit down, do sit down!" she kept repeating while fussing excessively with teacups, cookies, sugar in an ornate silver bowl, and lemon on an engraved silver stand. I thought perhaps she had invited us to meet her son and his family. But what was really on her mind was finding someone to whom she could sublet one room of her small apartment, and she wanted us to help her to look for such a person. She had, indeed, one more room, but it was small and unattractive, and the price she was hoping to get for it seemed to us far too high.

I looked around with interest, curious about her surroundings. The furniture in Henryka's apartment was very modest, obviously bought in old junk shops, but skillfully and tastefully arranged. The table was spread with an attractive cloth, a handwoven rug covered the couch, another rug hung on the wall above, and against this background was an image of the Virgin Mary, painted on metal.

"What is this holy picture, can you tell me?"

"You see, my dear," she began, and immediately excused herself for the way she was addressing me, claiming that the difference in our age fully justified her familiarity, "You see, my dear, this is a very interesting story."

She approached the bed and gently took the image in her large hand, now gnarled with rheumatism.

"The metal is from a tin can my Jasiek saved when he was in a prisoner-of-war camp. He made it into a sacred image, thinking of me. You see . . . ."

She now moved away from the bed and sat facing me with a thoughtful expression, pushing her lower lip forward and resting her chin on her hand glittering with rings, " . . . you see, we were such a close family, the 'holy family' people called us. One for all, as they say . . . ." She laughed. "Jasiek was twenty-four when we were separated. I did not see him for . . . how many years? I can never remember exactly. Yes, fifteen years . . . that's right, fifteen years . . . because it was in 1954, in winter, that I saw him again. And then, can you imagine, they came to the airport to meet me . . . and he takes this picture from his pocket and says: 'Mummy, all this time, all these years, I was with you in my every thought . . . .'"

|||

They had met again, after fifteen years, at the Monumental City airport in winter 1954, a few days before Christmas.

The snow was just beginning to fall when Jan and his family got out of the car.

"If it goes on like this," said Greta anxiously, "we'll never make it home."

"It's not that bad, we'll make it all right," Jan tried to calm her. The plane was late. They waited in the airport restaurant—Jan, Greta, and little Henry. The boy was seven, and he was wondering what present this new granny would bring him, this new granny of whose existence he learned only recently—and why should he have another granny if he already had one in Berlin, and she had only recently visited them? Jan helped Greta to take her coat off. She was wearing a red dress and looked remarkably young and slender—she had changed little in the nine years of their marriage. Her sensitive face blushed easily and showed freckles around her nose and on her forehead. She had pale, greenish eyes, easily dimmed with tears, and a look into them always told him how she was feeling. He saw now that she was frightened.

Of late, she had moved around the house without talking and often did not even answer him. Not that she did not want to, but she was so deep in her thoughts that she often did not even know what Jan said.

"Is she coming forever?" she asked.

"She is seventy, she is lonely, she is weary, she has nothing left in life. She would like to be with us until . . . ."

"No, with *you*," she said.

"No," he protested. "She always writes that Henry is her whole world, and she likes you very much, too. She knows, of course, how much I owe to you."

"So she writes . . . ," Greta answered.

Jan knew well how much he owed to Greta and often recalled it in his letters to his mother. He had met Greta shortly after he was freed from the POW camp. She was a quiet, shy girl of nineteen working at the UNRRA office where Jan was a frequent visitor at first and where he later worked as an interpreter because of his fluency in German. Greta was the daughter of a German industrialist, one of those who had passively resisted the Hitler regime and had been tolerated only because of their technical skills. She had grown up in the shadow of fear, in terror of imminent arrest and deportation to a concentration camp. The last months, the last weeks, of the war were the worst. She had lived through the bombings of Berlin and had escaped from their flaming house by jumping from a window. For a long time afterward, she had nightmares. During one long period of depression, she did not leave the house at all but sat in an armchair days on end, holding in her hands a book she could not even read.

Greta was attracted to Jan because he was different from other young men she had known. Her parents also liked him, and the father, seeing in him a future son-in-law, soon began to introduce him gradually into his business. And Jan fell in love with Greta. She was the first girl he had really liked since he left camp. He did not wish to go back to Poland. He had been liberated by the Allies, and he considered this to be good fortune and a fortuitous quirk of fate.

He did not hesitate long. Within a few months of their first meeting, they set the wedding date. In the meantime, he had gone through an apprenticeship in the precision instruments business of his future father-in-law. They agreed that the best thing for them would be to emigrate to the United States. When a Berlin firm decided to open a subsidiary in America, Greta's father, who knew the owners well, arranged for a well-paying American job for his son-in-law.

Jan's prewar law degree would not have been very helpful in the difficult task of building a new career in a foreign land. But now, properly introduced and recommended, he was several jumps ahead of other ex-POWs of similar background, who would have to invest long years in gaining new experience and advancing their new careers.

He wrote to his mother after the wedding and sent a picture of Greta, receiving in return a short and somewhat restrained blessing.

As a matter of fact, he never asked his mother openly in his letters what she thought about his marriage. What could she think of it, he asked himself? Every mother is a little jealous. I'm thirty, and if I want to get married and start a family . . . .

Sometimes, however, he was disturbed by a vague feeling of guilt and an ill-defined fear that he had broken some taboo, that he had crossed a line beyond which the path was not so certain and had to be trodden extremely cautiously. This sense of unease assailed him every time he thought about his mother, or his sister, who had died during the bombing of Warsaw, or his father, who had died during the German wartime occupation of Poland.

Waiting for the delayed plane at the airport, Jan wondered if he had acted wisely in bringing his mother from Poland. Immediately he upbraided himself sternly: "What else could I have done? Abandon this little old woman, widowed and bereaved and crushed by the long years of war? Leave her over there?"

"What are you thinking about?" asked Greta.

"The plane is late," he said.

"Perhaps she will not come?"

"Perhaps," he said, and for a moment he wished it were true.

"No, no!" he exclaimed, "What am I saying? She would have sent a wire."

At that moment the loudspeaker began to announce the arrival of the plane. Excited, forgetting their fears, they all got up and moved to the arrival gate. Outside the snow was falling thicker and faster. The runways and the hangars were covered with soft, pure down for a festive mood of welcome. They stood near the window, looking for Henryka. Deep in his coat pocket, Jan held the sacred image he had once made, wrapped in white tissue paper. He was deeply moved. He tried to imagine his mother's face and figure. She looked young in the snapshot she had sent him, but it was an old snapshot, perhaps even several years old. He strained to pick from among the passengers an old, slightly stooping figure in dark clothes, walking alone. He turned away from the window and said to Greta:

"I don't see her. I guess she didn't come after all."

But suddenly he heard her voice and he started, for it was the same voice he had heard from his room when he was a little boy, that had resounded from the corridor throughout the entire apartment, enfolding it, filling it.

"Weeeell at laaaast!"

Tall and erect, she stood facing them, an elegant lady in a fluffy brown fur coat and a fur hat, under which a few graying hairs could be seen. She was smiling, amused, talking lightly to a young man who carried her traveling bag.

She only said the first two words in Polish and then switched immediately to self-assured English, thanking the young man for his assistance and introducing him to Greta and Jan. Then she opened wide those arms in soft brown fur sleeves and embraced all three of them, surprising them slightly and leaving them breathless and astonished by her vigor.

Then, with a theatrical gesture, she pushed them away, held them at arm's length, and took a long look at them, each one separately and then all together, until they were embarrassed by the scene and the curious looks of passersby.

"At last," she said, smiling so touchingly that even Greta for a second yielded to the mood of family affection:

"Let me look at you, my dear, dear darlings . . . ."

Greta smiled uneasily and pulled her coat about her more tightly as the cold December air blew in through the open door.

"Jan," said Henryka. Her intense gaze swept over her son's face: the head, the thinning hair, the slightly rounded figure of a man who until yesterday, until a moment ago, had been to her a slim young man in an officer's uniform. She slid her furry sleeve under his arm.

"Now you lead me."

Greta and little Henry fell behind, and the distance between them grew steadily larger. This made Jan uneasy. He was reluctant to leave his mother, but did not wish to leave his wife behind either. He kept turning back and signaling Greta. He did not know whether he should give his mother the little image of the Virgin Mary now, or later, or perhaps never at all? Several times he reached into his pocket, but then it seemed to him that the picture did not belong to that moment or to the woman he had just met and who was his mother. He should have given her flowers instead. Only when they stood waiting for her baggage to arrive did he make up his mind. He took out the image wrapped in tissue paper and put it in her hand.

"This is what I wrote to you about, the little image I made when I was a prisoner . . . ."

She was moved. "My darling, let me see. But it's beautiful, beautiful. Let me kiss you. Oh, dear, there will be so much to tell, so much to talk about

. . . Just think, my son, only the two of us left, only two in the whole wide world . . . ."

Jan freed himself from her embrace and looked back. Greta stood leaning against the wall, holding little Henry by the hand. She seemed to him frail and plain, unsophisticated beside his magnificent, self-confident mother. He smiled and motioned them to come forward, but Greta shook her head, her lips tight and her green eyes, it seemed to him, dimmed with tears.

|||

"So, you see, he had kept it for me all those years," Henryka was saying to me.

"Does your son live near you now?" I inquired.

She gave me the name of the suburb where her son had his villa, as she called it.

"You probably want to know why I don't live there, don't you?"

"That is your business." I replied.

"Well, I don't live there. That's all there is to it. I did live there, for something like a year, but why should I be with them? I am an old hag, there is no point, no point at all. Perhaps I shall tell you one day how it was. The main rule in life is to count your blessings and keep your mouth shut."

She did not tell me more until I saw her in her second apartment. I guess it must have been three years later. I saw her a few times after we first met, but then she seemed to have disappeared. I heard her talk about going away, but I knew her so little that I did not even miss her.

"Whatever happened to Mrs. de Chatin?" I asked our mutual friend on the occasion of her next visit to Monumental City.

"Who knows? That woman's crazy. She is working somewhere as a lady's companion. I had a postcard from her. Instead of staying put, she's traipsing all around the States."

"She left rather suddenly . . . ."

"You can expect anything from her. All I know, from what my mother wrote to me, Henryka is a hard worker. I remember her in Warsaw, when she and her husband moved in next door to us after the Germans expelled them from western Poland. Imagine, she was actually supporting her husband and her daughter. Not only did she work, but she was doing all the housework as well. She washed bed sheets by hand and devised some sort of laundry system of her own."

On my return home one day, I found a message to call Henryka. I called her immediately.

"Hello?" she answered in a voice that had lost none of its thunder. She apologized for having disappeared so abruptly, but certain circumstances had forced her . . . .

"Never mind, all that is not important. I must, I simply must see you soon," she said.

Henryka's second apartment was in a comfortable suburban villa, a mansion set among azaleas and rhododendrons, with high windows reaching all the way down to the parquet floor. There was a nineteenth-century elegance in the arches of the roof, the *porte cochère,* the slender Victorian turrets with small windows that filtered the light of the sun and the moon. The spacious porch around it would have been ideal for summer dancing. The entire house was like a backdrop for Henryka's personality. The corner room, with an old magnolia tree outside touching the glass panes of the big window, was a perfect frame for her. So, I thought, she had found herself a suitable nest.

"Isn't this beautiful?" she said. "Wait. Look here. Just look here through the window. Isn't this magnificent? This is marvelous: a bright, sunny day outside, the birds singing, I can open my window and sit there, and what else could an old woman wish for? Sit tight and thank the Good Lord for His blessings, I always say."

"What about your son?" I asked.

Henryka busied herself making tea. She was moving about the spacious room that was her bedroom and her sitting room and her kitchen all rolled into one, where a large antique wardrobe reached almost to the moldings of the ceiling. There were paintings on the walls, portraits I had not seen before in her other apartment. But over her bed, covered with the same handwoven Polish kilim, there hung the same image of the Virgin Mary that Jan had painted for her in the POW camp.

"That's it," she answered my question at last, with her back turned. "You see, that's what worries me so much. He works so hard, too hard, in fact."

She sat next to me, and now I could see her better. In the course of the last three years she had not aged much, but somehow she had changed a great deal. The same deeply set, dark, and burning eyes, the same strong chin, the same vigorous cock of her head that belied her years. There was a vitality in her, a surging stream of life force that seemed almost frightening—not so much life itself but a passion for living at any price, for some impelling reason secretly known to her alone. She was no longer interested in earning a little extra money. Apparently her son was more affluent now, and apparently Henryka had accepted her dependence on him. Anyway, she had worked during the past few years and was now receiving a modest pension of her own, earned through her own efforts.

She did not tell me at that time why she had moved out of her son's home. This was to come later. She steered away from anything but generalities, punctuating vague phases with eloquent shrugs of her powerful shoulders.

To hear Henryka, her son was a giant. The precision instruments business of which, according to her, he was the top executive, had grown from success to success, all due to his efforts alone. He worked without a pause, and his many mysterious transactions (that Henryka would call "of extreme importance") required constant traveling. He traveled through all of Europe, flew to Asia, and visited Latin America. He stopped in Monumental City only briefly, saw his mother, then hurried to board another plane, to fly to still another country. He was busy, involved, important, and forever out of reach.

That afternoon, Henryka was more restless than usual. It was the time of the year when Monumental City is made particularly unpleasant by its gloomy weather. In late February, the cold is damp and piercing, the streets are covered with dirty slush, and even the sunniest optimists feel depressed and miserable.

Henryka complained of sleeping poorly, of having slipped on the sidewalk and bruised her hip painfully.

All the time she was talking, she kept glancing at the phone as if expecting it to ring at any moment. Several times she hinted that she was indeed expecting important news, and I could only guess that the news was coming from her son.

Despite the difference in our ages and despite the fact that, all in all, we did not see each other very often, somehow we grew much closer, Henryka and I. Ours was no longer a casual relationship, but rather a kind of conspiracy, a league of the initiated. Of the many members of this secret society, some I knew only slightly. Others I lost touch with long ago, yet news of important events in their lives or, indeed, news of their deaths would never be a matter of indifference to me. On the contrary, it would always prompt me to reflect upon their lives and upon my own life as well, for I was cut of much the same cloth. Sometimes I would wonder what it was that made this common link between people so patently different. The bond between us, I think, was that we all lived simultaneously in two worlds, not one, and that this split us irrevocably in half. No one who was not "one of us" could ever know us fully, because only one-half of our very selves ever showed—the other was kept in shadow. This cleft, with no sharp edge and indeed sometimes hardly noticeable, was the real danger point. There our madness crouched, ready to pounce at an opportune moment.

No one was really aware of this until, after some years away from the homeland, he had become, in part at least, a different person. It takes time to become acquainted with one's own duality. Sometimes it was possible to ignore it, to hide it, or even to triumph over it, but occasionally a searing flareup of madness would sweep away all reason.

"So you see," said Henryka, "we decided to be patient and wait." She did not even explain the "we" in this conspiratorial alliance. These things are perfectly clear to members of the secret society. I knew "we" included Henryka and her son, but not Greta. Greta, her son, and her family were on the other side.

"Patience, my dear, and time. Time will solve all problems and truth will win. We should not force the issue. We do have a plan, and—but I do not wish to talk about it. Still, I have high hopes."

"What sort of plan?"

"Well," she smiled mysteriously, "there are certain things I'd rather not mention—as yet. All I can tell you . . . ," she suddenly resolved to add, " . . . is that it can't ever be patched up again."

She sat in her chair, deep in thought, all wrapped up in her schemes. I was still groping for some meaning, when suddenly she decided to confess, briefly and desperately, the whole truth, as if prompted by some secret wave that had swept her mind clear.

"You see, their marriage is not really all it should be. When I arrived on that wintry day, straight from the airport, everything bright with the new snow, God knows I had the best intentions. We went home . . . ."

It was a bright suburban home, painted white, with white drapes in the windows and wooden floors smelling of fresh wax. Henryka took her fur coat off in her room, which was to be her home from then on. She unpacked the gifts she had brought, and looked once more at the holy picture Jan had given her. Her mind went back to the years when she and her husband and their daughter, and later only she and her daughter, and later still only she alone, had waited for Jan to return home.

She went downstairs, thinking of all she was going to tell them, of how much she was going to add to their store of memories, and of how they were going to gather round her to listen. She walked into the living room but heard their voices coming from the kitchen, all talking together, even the little boy. They were talking in German. Jan was explaining something to Greta, and she was answering plaintively. Henryka understood immediately they were talking about her. She stood there for a little while and then realized that she was trembling, shaking, unable to control her face any longer and that she was going to dissolve in a flood of tears.

She ran upstairs quickly, threw herself on the bed, and burst into uncontrollable sobs, stifling her moans in the pillow. Long-forgotten memories now assailed her from all sides. All of 1939 came back to her: the expulsion from their apartment in Poznań; the German order to move east; the provisional evacuation camp out in the open, surrounded by barbed wire; their journey to Warsaw in overcrowded trains; the long lines for permits of all sorts; the lack of accommodations (they'd had no place of their own for a long time); her husband's illness; her husband's death; the Warsaw Uprising; flight from a burning, collapsing house; her daughter's death under the rubble. And all the time, the never-ceasing, deep, painful fear. The sound track of these images moving swiftly in her brain was always the same: it was in German, the same language her son, her daughter-in-law, and her grandson were using at this moment down in the kitchen.

"This is absurd," she scolded herself. "I knew all about it. I knew it all the time and I was resigned to it. I understood." But she was pleading with herself in vain, and the despair that took hold of her could not be denied. No argument could calm her mind or soothe her sense of loss, the loss of her own self.

Downstairs, they thought she was exhausted by her journey and had fallen asleep. She got up finally and washed her face. Moving around the clean little room, so beautifully polished by Greta's busy hands, she knew something had snapped inside her, something had died, and something else was born in its place.

"I have lived too long," she said to Jan when he came to check on her. "It would have been better had I been hit by a bomb and never lived to see this day."

"But , mother," exclaimed Jan. "You knew. For goodness sake, if Greta found out . . . God forbid! She'd be heartbroken!"

"You must not tell her," she ordered him. "I have come to terms with it in my own mind. It's a heartache, certainly, but what of it? I shall just cry and weep and sleep it off."

Jan left her bewildered. He had expected anything but this kind of reaction. The old dilemma came back to him, a feeling of guilt for having married Greta. But guilt toward whom? It wasn't Greta's fault. The poor girl had suffered a great deal herself. Perhaps he was wrong in bringing his mother over? Perhaps he should have cut himself off from the past once and for all?

|||

After that initial shock, Henryka pulled herself together. She felt a surge of new strength as if she were entering a new life—not her eighties.

She had decided that her coming to the United States was ordained by fate. She had felt since the very beginning that some danger was threatening Jan and that now she only had to be watchful and she would save him. What sort of a danger that was, she still did not know. It took the vague shape of unfriendly forces that she alone could overcome with the strength of her own will. It was, therefore, of the greatest importance to act immediately.

First of all, she had decided to win Greta over, to make her pliable to her own will by gaining her friendship, and thus to forestall the lurking dangers.

"I don't believe in destiny, I don't believe in premonitions. It's all old wives' tales and nothing else. Every problem can be turned around by the will. One has to will life."

Henryka fell silent, absorbed in her thoughts. She got up and began pacing the room, apologizing that her still-painful hip did not let her sit in one place for long. Perhaps she was just wondering if she had not told me too much? Her movements were restless, sometimes she stopped and listened. "Just a minute . . . did I hear the phone ring?"

I saw that she was agitated, even exasperated, and that her mind was somewhere else. I decided to leave, but she was horrified.

"No, no, for heaven's sake, don't go. Would you like some more tea, or a cookie, or perhaps a glass of wine?" she coaxed me. "Wait, wait a little."

Perhaps to stop me from leaving, or perhaps thinking she could trust me now, she began to talk again.

"It started like this, between Greta and me. I came to the kitchen, I wanted to help. She was doing the dishes, and I took a cloth to dry them and I said: 'My dear child, I would like to talk to you from my very heart. You are my son's wife and so you are like a daughter to me. Why do you address me formally, as Mrs. de Chatin? Call me Mother.' She glanced at me and said 'No.' 'Why?' I said. God be my witness, I had the best intentions. 'Because,' she said, 'we can only have one mother. My mother is in Berlin.' So I said 'Greta' again, and I even put my arm around her shoulders, but she did not like being touched and drew back. 'My child,' I said, 'I could never take the place of your real mother and I would not even try, but you belong to our family now and it's as though I have two children, isn't that right?' She shook her head, 'If you prefer, I can call you Henryka, but never Mother.' 'Well,' I said to myself, 'this will never do; no snotty little whippersnapper is going to call me by my first name.' So we could not come to an agreement on that, and it was the same with everything else. Henry is a bright little lad, quite exceptionally gifted, so I began to teach him Polish. Greta was furious: the boy's mind will be ruined, a third language will confuse him, it is too early, English and German are quite enough. Jan tried to persuade her but to no avail. I was at a loss what to do with myself in that household. There wasn't much to talk about with Greta. When Jan would get home, after dinner the two of us would often spend the whole evening in my room, just talking."

"Would it have been better, perhaps, for you to go back?"

"Go back?" She sprang up. "Back to what?" she said scornfully. "My place is with Jan. He needs me."

Henryka gave me a hostile look, as though I had gone too far over the line into the world only she and her son belonged to, into their own intimate world.

She got up immediately and went over to her small electric range. I could see her strong, straight back, her broad hips and big legs planted so firmly, so securely on the ground, and I thought: "What life, what fire rages inside this human frame so close to its end and still so full of plans for the future?" I could see she burned with an inner flame, planning, plotting, scheming things only hinted at in our conversation.

When she turned around, she was smiling. She was the same old Henryka, with her slightly trembling head and the benevolent smile of a person who had lived through everything, who understood and forgave everything.

"You see," she was saying, "I do not have anyone left, no one to go back to. And why should an old woman keep going back and forth? I always call myself an old hag. First thing in the morning I prod myself: 'Get going, you old hag.' You know, I can get really annoyed at my own clumsiness."

Now I was smiling, too, for I knew what I was witnessing was just the recitation of a formula refined by constant repetition over nearly eighty years. The real Henryka, the one who came to life on that first night after her arrival, sat deeply hidden, enclosed in the spider webs of her schemes.

"One must be patient. You see, we've decided to wait patiently. We have a plan, but I do not wish to talk about it now. The main thing is to leave it all to time, to circumstances. As I always say: patience is all."

Her thin eyelids descended to cover one half of her dark eyes. She leaned back in her armchair, rocking gently, smiling mysteriously and savoring the approaching triumph.

Still, Henryka had moments, and perhaps even days, of doubt. Most often, the doubt would overtake her in her sleep. She was defenseless then, and deprived of the willpower that gave her strength during her waking hours, when she was able to muster the courage to face her future.

One day she told me about her dream.

It was spring again, and the magnolia outside her window was a cloud of deep pink. Henryka was feeling better that day. Fresh flowers filled the vases in her room: from her son. She was excited, laughing, gesticulating, bubbling with gaiety about spring and about the new neighbors who had moved into the apartment below hers.

"What extraordinary people they are! Such a loving family. Their son and his wife and children always come from New York to visit them. They are Quakers, you see, and only yesterday they took me for a ride in their car, out of town to where these Quakers have their big house. On top of the hill there is this charming little cemetery . . . ."

"And what about your son?"

"Well, you see, that's the problem. He is away again. I expect him to be back any day now. Before he left . . . you see, these flowers . . . The dear boy can't do enough for me . . . ."

"You feel better today," I said.

"Yes, in a way," she agreed. "But I had a dream . . . I'll show you something first."

She went to the wardrobe, and the heavily carved doors squeaked open. Henryka leaned forward, half-disappearing inside, and fished out a large, rectangular piece of cardboard. Lifting it with both her hands and drawing back coquettishly, she said to me:

"Look at this. This is my dream."

I got up and moved back a few paces to get a better look at the watercolor she was holding.

"Yes, yes," she nodded, amused by my expression of surprise. "I painted this myself. Sometimes I paint now, just for myself. It's marvelous therapy. I even talked Jan into taking a course in sculpture. He is extremely gifted, you know."

It was a strange and frightening picture, a tangle of many different shades of green, from vivid to dark, that transitioned gradually to a deep, dull black. Only when I listened to her explanation did I understand the meaning of the painting. Henryka propped her watercolor against the wardrobe and, touching the edge of the cardboard from time to time, tapping it with a beringed finger, or caressing it with her palm, she said:

"I had this dream, you see. I am in the woods. Everything is lush and green and smelling of sap. You know how I love nature, how I long for forests like this one. I keep on walking. The trees are tall, their crowns almost joining above me. I'm in a tunnel of green the sun can hardly penetrate. I walk on and on—and suddenly this abyss opens right in front of me. Look here. Can you see it? Right there . . . I feel I am falling in. So I grab some branches—these here, can you see them? I hold on for dear life and try desperately to haul myself up, but everything comes apart in my hands, and I feel I am sinking faster and faster. I begin to clutch at the sides of this ghastly hole, I claw at them, still falling and dreadfully frightened. Where am I going? I am going to hit the bottom, I am going to sink. Should I call out for help? Falling, falling into this yawning hollow that is pulling me in faster and faster, at an insane speed . . . cannot even catch my breath in this whirlpool. And then I woke up."

|||

That fall I left Monumental City. More than two years elapsed before I returned again. During these years we exchanged occasional letters with Henryka de Chatin and received Christmas greetings from her. Last Christmas we even received two cards from Henryka—obviously she was getting a little confused and could not remember, as very old people sometimes cannot, what took place yesterday or an hour or even a moment ago. In New York I saw our friend who, many years before, had brought Henryka and me together. I told her that Henryka and I had become good friends and that I had heard from her recently.

"You mean she is still alive?" she exclaimed.

I resented the remark and felt sure Henryka would take umbrage, too. "Why shouldn't she be alive?" I said. "She has more strength and more stamina than many young people."

"Well, after what happened . . . ."

"What did happen?" I asked.

"A dreadful tragedy . . . her son . . . I heard about it from someone who just came from Monumental City."

That evening I called Monumental City. Henryka must have been out, for no one answered the ring. Only after 10:00 p.m. did she finally answer.

"Hello?" Her voice sounded the same: stately, powerful, and composed.

"Oh, it's you my dear." She was very pleased. "Just imagine! What a disaster. Jan was in this car accident. Didn't I write you about it? That's me, always forgetting everything. It happened just a short time ago. He is now in a hospital, yes, unconscious, yes, but making progress, getting on well, the doctors are performing miracles, everything in their power . . . ."

She also told me she was no longer living in that suburban villa. She had moved very recently, having found a bargain, a real bargain.

Henryka's third apartment was in a modern building, run by a private benevolent foundation for senior citizens in reduced circumstances who could no longer afford a home of their own or provide for themselves. Henryka had been dreaming about this kind of home for a long time. Her second apartment, the one in the suburban villa, charming though it was, had its own drawbacks. The high, winding stairs were too much for Henryka, and she'd had no kitchen of her own, no bathtub to relax and soak in.

Walking through this hotel for old people, I felt as if I were sailing in a large, white, silent ship rolling gently and quietly toward a secure port where the passengers would disembark wordlessly without looking back. The occupants moved like shadows along the walls. They passed by me carefully, guardedly, pausing at the huge glass entrance doors to look out on the soft freshness of the evening at the end of a hot autumn day.

Henryka was waiting for me on the eighth floor, at the elevator. She opened her arms wide to hug me, and her embrace was strong, too powerful really. It felt like a hammerlock I was eager to escape.

"Look at my hair," she was saying. "Isn't it dreadful? It is all coming out. I look awful in those cheap wigs. I did try them on, but I can't bear to look at myself in one. An old hag, that's what I am, an old hag." She did not say one word about her son's accident. I was expecting tears, a broken and despairing old woman, but Henryka—though she had, indeed, aged considerably—was somehow even more vigorous. She moved briskly about her little apartment, showing me its luxuries: the tiny kitchen, the walk-in closet, the bathroom, the two telephones. I admired and praised it all, but I missed the magnolia tree outside the window, and the stucco ceiling, and the creaking, ancient wardrobe.

"Wait, wait, I have not shown you everything yet."

"But how is your son?"

"I'll tell you in a moment, just a second, look, look here . . . ."

She pulled a cord on the drapes, and, through the huge window, the width of the entire wall, the early evening entered the room. The panorama of the city in the distance was a hazy sketch of roofs and church spires, of trees already marked yellow and orange by the early fall, and of a big red sun setting in purple clouds. It was one of those enchanted sunsets over the bay when the sun's disk seems so close that we imagine we could run outside and reach for it with our hands, over there, just behind that house, behind that tree, hanging from that branch.

She was looking at me with an expression of triumph, as if she had just unveiled before me her own painting. But then she sat down immediately, tired and oddly resigned, and she did not protest my making the tea and putting the cookies on the silver plate.

"It was in December," she said, "Soon after Christmas. It must have been just before New Year's Eve."

"Jan came to wish me a happy New Year. His marriage—well, no point hiding it—was not really going well. Greta had gone to Berlin to spend the entire summer with her parents and did not come back until school started in September. In the meantime, I cooked here for Jan as well as I could, and he often took me home to their place. He told me this and that, the marriage was not working out at all. I could see that things were pretty bad. Jan would relax with me, but when she came back in the fall it all flared up again. He would come here and tell me how it was. I know perfectly well how hard he worked and how much he invested in that home for them and how much he loved it. A fine kettle of fish . . . What was I saying? He came to see me, it was late at night, it was raining, it was snowing—you know, that horrid, treacherous weather . . . ."

Jan de Chatin was fifty-four that winter, and to those who did not see him through his mother's eyes he appeared balding, rather portly, slightly over-weight. He had intelligent, dark eyes underlined with puffy circles, and a prominent nose jutting forth from a round face with an incipient double chin and a red flush common to those suffering from hypertension. He looked like a tired man, and his complexion, his puffed-up eyes, and his red nose showed that alcohol, so indispensable at business meetings and official parties, simply did not agree with him. He was not so much a quiet man as a self-controlled one. But during the last few years, especially since his mother's arrival, he had become touchy and irritable, because he had to soothe and justify endlessly to appease Greta's jealousy of his mother or to satisfy his mother's demands on his time and attention. His own son, of whom he saw very little, in fact, was somehow slipping away from him. They could not find a common language, and, before he realized it, they had become strangers, treating each other with purely formal politeness and expressions of family affection. Though Jan found it hard to admit, he could relax best with his mother. With her, he could speak openly and in Polish, which, in itself, reduced the tension, like taking off a starched collar after a formal dinner at which one did not feel at ease.

It was a wet December night. Sleet and snow were sticking to the wind-shield. Jan de Chatin parked his car in the space outside the house where his mother lived. His mother had moved there only recently, barely two weeks before Christmas. He had managed to obtain that apartment for her, thanks to their doctor, who was open in his admiration for Henryka, for her cour-age, her energy, and her personality.

Henryka was waiting for her son at the door of her suite on the eighth floor. She stretched her arms and took his face in her hands, kissing his cheeks, overflowing with tenderness and love. Jan kissed both her hands, took her arm, and entered her suite.

"Are you going to eat something?" she asked.

"No, no, don't bother."

"But I can see you are frozen to the bone," she was fussing. "Would you like some coffee perhaps?"

"I brought a bottle of cognac for you."

"Oh, darling, how you do remember that I sometimes like a little glass of something. All right, shall we have some?"

Jan nodded and opened the bottle, pouring a small glass for his mother and one for himself. He sat down in the armchair, and immediately Henryka was at his side with a cushion for him.

"How is everything?" she asked, lowering her voice. Jan sighed.

"I know, I know, you don't have to tell me."

"I am worried about the boy. He will soon be twenty. He smashed that car not long ago . . . I didn't say anything . . . not really . . . Thank God he wasn't hurt . . . ."

"Thank God, indeed," she murmured, nodding vigorously.

"But he never comes to me, never talks to me . . . I don't know a thing about that college of his."

"You see, Jan, you must be very, very patient . . . ."

"Mother, listen . . . ," Jan poured himself another glass of cognac. "It's not that simple . . . ."

"Of course. Of course, it isn't," she agreed again, closely watching his face and worrying, for he looked not only tired and troubled but as though he suffered from a sorrow far deeper than Greta's nagging and their everyday niggling spats.

Henryka knew what it was, for did they not feel alike? Hadn't she learned in her more than eighty years to read people's hearts and dreams? She knew that all paths, straight or twisting, that all roads and byways, whether wide or narrow, lead always to the same goal. Did not all the desires and all the longings and all the dreams for the future converge on that same point? Only fools could dupe themselves into thinking that their ambitions and hopes are an end to themselves, for nothing can ever take the place of that which is the final mark of every human desire. All feelings merge into one single desperate wish: to survive, to pass on one's own identity, not to die entirely.

"It's not at all that simple," Jan said again. "I feel as if I had no son. He spends all his time with his mother. They speak only German together, and I . . . I am . . . ."

Henryka shook her head, still powerfully set on her muscular neck, and trembled. They had taken away from her son—from her Jan, the only child she had left—his most precious right. They had robbed him of the only treasure that makes life meaningful: they had denied him the joy of seeing himself reflected in his own child.

"Oh, my God, my dear God . . . ," she moaned.

"You see," Jan said resignedly, "It preys on my mind. Sometimes I think, perhaps, I should have been with him more often, but I was always traveling, always on the go . . . ."

"But you were working," she said anxiously, trying to soothe him. "They should have understood that."

"They didn't. They just didn't understand it. It's not so easy to explain to a small child, is it? And now, well, now it's too late."

"Wait! Wait!" she exclaimed in her deep voice, "It's never too late. We have our plans, don't we? Be calm, be patient, and when she leaves . . . Just be patient.

"I'll go now, mother," he said.

"All right," she agreed, for she felt exhausted from their talk. She embraced him and hugged him with those strong arms that never brooked any resistance. He yielded limply, passively, too passively, in fact, and it frightened her.

"Now, Jan, what is it? What's wrong?"

"What can be wrong?" He shrugged his shoulders. "That's life. Just take care of yourself, and if you want anything, give me a ring. You'd better call me at the office . . . ."

"Yes, of course, I know, the office . . . ." Again she attempted to calm him.

"I'll drop in again soon, perhaps the day after tomorrow."

"My dear boy," she said, stroking his cheek, "take care of yourself. Don't work too hard."

Henryka de Chatin was sitting in her armchair with her hands crossed in her lap. I thought she had dozed off. Her dark eyes, now seeming bigger than ever, were surrounded by a fine net of purple veins etched on her temples, her eyelids, and at the base of her nose. Her complexion had darkened and was covered with scattered brown splotches like coffee stains. It was as if I were watching a gnarled log being devoured by fire, fiercely blazing, finally transformed into pure flame, yet still part of a once-living tree.

"How did it happen?" I asked.

"He parked his car and was just getting out . . . ," she spoke in a voice devoid of emotion. "It was soon after he left my place. I don't know, maybe he went downtown to get something. Because it happened downtown. That man hit him, just hit him. People drive like madmen. Jan always said: driving carefully is not enough, you have to watch out for others. Dreadful, dreadful. But, you know . . . ," her voice grew more vigorous now, " . . . our doctor notified me immediately, because Greta called him, and they took him to Percival Norris. I went over instantly, and after that I went to see him twice a day. For two weeks he was seldom conscious. I saw her there, too."

"Greta?"

"Yes."

"In such tragic circumstances people draw closer . . . ."

"Not really," she shrugged. "Not necessarily."

"Is he still at the hospital?"

"Of course not. The insurance didn't want to pay any longer. He was transferred to another hospital, yes, he needs further treatment. It'll take time. He still can't walk."

"Where is he now? Which hospital?" Henryka did not answer. She tried to change the subject.

"Now you, tell me all about yourself," she insisted.

"Which hospital?" I asked again, aware that Henryka was trying to hide something from me.

She got up and lowered the blinds. Outside it was already dark. Without looking at me, she mumbled:

"Jan is in Pine Grove."

She waited for my reaction, then turned to me and said:

"They are taking fantastic care of him there, you know. The doctors just outdo themselves to help him. The nurses like him too. They say he is an exceptional patient, simply exceptional."

Henryka went to see her son at Pine Grove two or three times a week. It was quite an expedition for her, and she had to prepare for it a day ahead. To get to Pine Grove, she had to take the city bus. On some Saturdays or Sundays, friends—maybe those Quakers she had met at her second apartment—would drive her there.

Henryka dressed carefully, as usual. She took fruit for Jan in a handbag and rode the elevator downstairs.

"I am going to the hospital," she told the receptionist at the desk in the lobby, where several office girls from the administration usually worked. One of them, whose duty was to keep track of the residents of the home, stopped her.

"Mrs. de Chatin," she said in a low voice, "please do not ride the bus alone."

Henryka laughed, "What can happen to me? I am not fragile. I shall not break into small pieces."

"Don't you remember what happened last week? Some people had to bring you back here."

"People are kind," she said, but the girl frowned.

"You were completely lost, you were wandering the streets alone . . . ."

"Oh, yes." Henryka felt suddenly apologetic. "I remember now. I had completely forgotten."

"At your age," said the girl, "you must be careful. I warned you, if it ever happens again . . . ."

"But that was only once, and these people who brought me back here were so nice . . . ." Henryka was on the defensive.

"Now you are forgetting again." The girl was angry. "And what happened two weeks ago? That's right, two weeks ago, when you fell in the street and somebody brought you back here in his car. I've warned you before that we can keep only those people who can look after themselves. I am warning you again."

"Oh, dear," Henryka was really upset now. "I am very, very sorry. I completely forgot about it. I will be very careful, I promise."

But as she was walking out, pushing the big glass revolving door, she had already forgotten. She was muttering: "That old maid . . . never had any children of her own . . . what can she know how a mother's heart feels?"

Head held high, a soft turban wrapped around her thinning hair, Henryka walked to the nearest bus stop.

Her exchanges with the receptionist, her concerns of yesterday or the week before, promptly slipped out of her mind. She simply could not remember, could not retain, these things in her mind. Sometimes she could not recall what she had eaten an hour before, or whether she had eaten at all. Some days, she could not even remember why Jan was in the hospital. Only one thing she knew for sure, only one thought never left her, awake or asleep, whether she was tossing on her bed at night or rising in the morning to face another dreadful day, feeling the pitiless ache of old age in all her bones: Jan was in the hospital. Jan still could not walk. He was . . . Oh God, oh God! Jan was . . . She could not bring herself to think about it in her waking hours. But sometimes, in her sleep, she could cry aloud and wail so despairingly that her next-door neighbor would knock on the wall.

Now she sat on a bench to wait for her bus. Other passengers arrived, black women with big bosoms and big bottoms who, like her, were going to Pine Grove to see their relatives. The bus driver knew her by now. She was so different from other travelers, a well-dressed lady not quite belonging to this age, her arms jingling with bracelets, who addressed the driver as "my dear man" and thanked him for what was simply his job.

The hospital was in the suburbs. It took about an hour to get there. At one time there had been fields and woodland between the hospital and Monumental City, and traces of them were still visible on the hillsides, but the city had come nearer to Pine Grove. Even so, when the bus left the side road and entered the hospital grounds, Henryka had a cold feeling of crossing the line between two worlds.

The state hospital, known as Pine Grove because it was located in a small suburb of that same name, was a large complex of old brick buildings, now blackened with time. Despite the administration's efforts to modernize the facilities and to add new, brighter buildings, Pine Grove retained the dark aura common to the many mental hospitals once called, at the time of their founding, asylums for the insane. It sheltered many patients who had entered the hospital while still in their teens and who would never, to the end of their lives, leave its grounds. Those who were unable to pay the costs of a private psychiatric clinic, who could not afford the luxury of a private mental hospital, or whose funds to pay for psychiatric care had run out, were sent to Pine Grove.

After the accident on that wet December night, when Jan de Chatin was run over by a car, he lost more than the use of his legs. The protracted loss of consciousness had affected his brain so drastically that his mind had regressed and he had become a feeble, whimpering child, totally irresponsible. But, from time to time, some glimmer of awareness struck him, and then he wanted to flee, to go back, to go back home.

Henryka got out at the main administration building. From there she still had a long walk to Jan's ward. It was late summer, still hot, and she was exhausted when she reached her destination.

The one-story building of red brick was a little more modern than the others. Its windows were barred, and the entrance door was locked. Henryka rang the bell. The nurse who opened the door knew Henryka from her previous visits, and she led her into a small lobby with a Coca-Cola vending machine.

Henryka was hot and thirsty, and the nurse helped her to get a bottle from the machine, then waited for her to drink and to catch her breath. "How—how is he today?" Henryka asked between the gulps, cooling her hands on the bottle. "Did anyone come? Did he have any visitors?"

"No," the girl shook her head. "Only that attorney . . . ."

"Oh, yes, yes," Henryka nodded.

"Did you know his wife is divorcing him?"

"So now she'll get everything? The house, the car, everything?"

"You'd better ask that attorney."

The nurse was a young girl. She was not wearing a white uniform, but an ordinary summer dress, as is usual in many psychiatric hospitals.

"After your last visit he was very upset," she said.

"Why?"

"We had to restrain him again."

"Oh, my God, why?" Henryka was appalled.

"He was very upset, he wanted to run away, to go back home."

"Which home?" asked Henryka. The nurse looked at her mindfully.

"What do you mean, which home?"

"Because at first he wanted to go back to his old home in Poland, he told me so, and he asked me why daddy hadn't come . . . ."

"No," said the nurse. "Where that's concerned, he is a little better. He's now coming back to the present time."

"That's a good sign, isn't it?"

"You must try not to upset him this time."

Henryka gave the nurse a hostile glance. The girl did not look like a hospital nurse at all: that long hair, and why didn't she wear a white uniform the way she ought to? Snotty little girl, she wants to teach me, to tell me how my son and I . . . .

But she smiled knowingly and nodded approvingly, as if she were the one instructing the girl how to treat a patient.

"That's right, no excitement. Rest, quiet. The most important thing is to be calm and relaxed."

With one of her keys the nurse opened another door, this one leading into a corridor. A heavy wave of stale air hit them, the smell of many human bodies in close quarters. From the main corridor, other corridors ran at right angles, each one closed by heavy doors. The walls and the floors were tiled. Along the main passage were the hospital offices. The nurse and Henryka turned right and stopped at a door leading to a side corridor. The nurse opened it with another of her keys. The passage was lit by an electric bulb. Only a little daylight came from a window at the far end, where another nurse sat behind a desk in a glass booth. She was wearing a starched white uniform and a peaked white cap. At the window where she dispensed medicines there swayed an unruly line of silent figures. They stretched out their hands for pills, clutched them firmly, and moved away from the booth, pensive and detached, only to stop close by, leaning against the wall or sitting down or even lying on the floor.

They were wearing pajamas, robes, shirts, and slacks. They were only half-dressed, and all looked stunned or in a daze. Henryka and the nurse stepped over someone lying stretched out on the floor, blocking the passage. The man did not even move, gazing fixedly at the ceiling. Several patients became excited by the appearance of the nurse. They walked over to her, tugged at her dress, fawned on her like little children craving attention. One of them came to the nurse and began to babble something, stuttering, explaining haltingly something terribly important, terribly urgent. She turned to him gently and disengaged herself from his grasp.

"Not now," she said. "I'm busy now, Tom."

The two women turned another corner, where the corridor was almost empty. The doors to the rooms were topped with small barred windows. The nurse stopped in front of one of these doors and turned her key in the lock.

Jan de Chatin was sitting in a wheelchair, his back turned to the barred window behind him, which admitted but scant daylight. He was wearing gray hospital pajamas. He did not move. He did not seem to have noticed the door opening or his mother coming in. His eyes were fixed on one distant point beyond the green painted wall of his room. From one corner of his half-open mouth, a slow trickle of saliva was running onto his chin. His hands rested limply on his knees. His hair had turned gray. His yellow, sagging face showed traces of the accident and his debilitating sickness.

"Hi, Jan," called the nurse. She leaned over him and touched his shoulder gently. "Look who's here! You have a visitor."

Jan de Chatin slowly turned his gaze toward his mother, and his glazed eyes showed a sign of understanding.

"Jasiek, my boy," said Henryka in her usual loud, solicitous tone of voice. "How are you, my poor darling?"

The nurse stopped at the door. "Half an hour," she said. "And if you need me, just ring the bell."

"Good evening, Mommy," Jan said obediently. It was the voice of a well-mannered little boy. He kissed her extended hand, heavy with rings and marked with brown age spots.

"I brought you some peaches," she fussed. "Do you want one? Do you want me to peel one for you?"

He did not answer, but Henryka began to peel a peach with the pen-knife she had brought with her.

"Here you are, eat it up, look what a beautiful peach," she coaxed. "Eat, for goodness sake, eat it, you must get better."

"Thank you, Mommy," he said. He chewed the fruit obediently but unwillingly, still staring at some distant point beyond the wall.

Suddenly he spat out a half-chewed piece. Tears began to roll from his blurred eyes.

"What is it? What's wrong, my darling?" She wiped his tears with her handkerchief.

"I want to go home!" he sobbed, "Home!"

"My dearest," she began. She hugged his rigid shoulders and stroked his cheek, covered with gray stubble. "You have no home, you don't have a home any more. But you must get well. You must make an effort . . . with all your will . . . ."

He looked at her uncomprehendingly. Impatiently he pushed away her hands.

"Home," he repeated. "I want to go home . . . ."

"My boy, my dearest boy, my little Jan." She stroked his motionless hands. "There is no home. Please, you must understand. There is no home left. You must make an attempt . . . you must do all in your power to . . . ."

"All right, yes, Mother, yes," he said, obedient again.

"Now, my boy, my good little boy, now eat your peach. Force yourself to eat. It will do you good." She pushed the fruit into his mouth again. "Do try."

Jan shoved her away so violently that she very nearly lost her balance, but managed somehow to lean against the narrow bed near the wall. With a savage jerk he flung the peach away, his face contorted in a hideous, tearful scowl.

"I want to go home!" he sobbed and howled desperately. "Home! Home!" He began to tear his clothes, tried to get up from the wheelchair, pounded his immobile legs furiously with his fists and wailed without words, no longer weeping , but howling an insane, terrifying cry.

Before Henryka could press the bell, the nurse and an orderly ran into the room. The girl gave her a reproving look and shook her head.

"Wait outside," she said.

Henryka walked out obediently. She saw the doctor arrive hastily, his white coat open. She tried to intercept him.

"You can see for yourself," he shrugged in passing. "We are trying to do everything we can." He walked on, leaving her leaning against the wall, waiting.

"They are doing everything possible," she kept telling herself. "Everything possible. One must have confidence and patience. Yes, patience ... everything will turn out all right."

The nurse came out of the room. Henryka could hear Jan sobbing quietly now. But there were also other sounds, as if of a struggle, as if he were trying to free himself. The nurse walked ahead, opening the many doors, each with a different key.

"We gave him an injection. He will be quiet now," she said.

"Does he suffer a great deal?" asked Henryka.

"Sometimes," the girl said. "And sometimes such a state is better than the real world."

"But is he improving? Is he getting better?"

"We are doing everything possible. Perhaps you shouldn't come again this week."

"Why?" Henryka was alarmed. "Why is that?"

"Perhaps next week, and ... don't tell him he has no home to go back to."

"What should I tell him then? It's true. He has no home."

"Let him get well first."

"That's right, you're so right. He must get well first, that's the most important."

|||

That night Henryka walked with me to the elevator.

"That hospital . . . ," she was saying, "He gets marvelous medical care in that hospital. They even say to me: do not come, we are looking after him like a mother would!"

She looked around the bright, spacious corridor, full of light, of flowers, all shining floors and peaceful silence.

"How do you feel here?" I asked.

"Great!" she exclaimed. "Only," she lowered her voice, "you understand, one thing is missing. I wish Jan were here with me."

She leaned against the wall, her gray head gently shaking with that slight trembling she no longer could control. She put both hands to her lips and sent me two big kisses.

The next time I saw her, she was in the hospital. During one of her trips to visit Jan she had fallen and had broken her hip. The home for senior citizens would not allow her to remain there, and she did not know where she was going to live after she left the hospital. She was terribly worried about that. When I came to visit her, she looked feverish and did not recognize me at first. She grasped my hand.

"I am worried, I am terribly worried about Jan. He is in such pain . . . ."

When I got home, I called Henryka's grandson and told him about her accident, asking him to visit her in the hospital. I did not think she would recuperate. But she did, and the next time I saw her, she was in her fourth apartment.

Henryka's fourth apartment was downtown, in a building across from the oldest synagogue in town. Her windows looked out on a small green square with the statue of a soldier. One had to climb high steps before ringing a bell in the heavy old front door. The house had five floors and once had been owned by a wealthy citizen who left it to charity. As soon as the bell rang, the heavy doors would open slightly, and one immediately saw the faces of old people, white and black, men and women, peering with childish curiosity and chattering in thin, shrill voices. They lined both sides of the entrance hall—some on crutches, some in wheelchairs, the women looking fragile like unfeathered baby chicks—all gaping at the visitor, for it was seldom they saw strangers in this old people's home run by the city.

Henryka occupied a bed in the corner of a large room. Propped up against her pillows, she had gathered around her, on a night table and a little shelf, all that she had left in the world: family photographs, the image of the Virgin (once made by Jan from a tin can), some crumbling cookies, and a bottle of eau de Cologne. Her lunch tray, brought by a nurse who then had forgotten to feed her, remained untouched. She was feeling a little better, but her hip still bothered her, and she was feverish. She was thinner and pitifully shrunken. She looked at me and smiled.

"See what's become of the old hag?"

She told me Jan seemed to be a little better, but still suffering a great deal, and that she hoped to get better herself and then . . . .

"As soon as I am strong enough," she said, but without any great conviction.

I dreaded going to that old people's home. We would make it a family project to go there at Christmastime and then again at Easter. But these visits left me so depressed for several days after that I simply avoided seeing her.

The last time we saw her must have been some six months before she died. She had been moved to another room, and, even before we got there, we heard her loud, impatient voice from the corridor. As we entered, Henryka was sitting on a chamber pot and shouting at the nurse, scolding her sharply. She was wearing a skimpy nightdress, her thin legs showing from underneath.

"They say," she immediately complained, "that I'm showing off my legs on purpose."

A stout, lame black woman was complaining to the nurse about Henryka.

Henryka had shrunk so much that I could recognize her only by the large, strong nose, the burning dark eyes, and the determined chin. She was wearing a ridiculous little white cap, which was a sort of uniform for all the old women in the home, but which did not suit her at all, for it was symbolic of a docile and mellow old age, while she looked more like a huge bird of prey. Incongruously decked out in the lacy white cap, she surveyed us briefly, cocking her head to the side, before she nodded that, yes, she recognized us, of course.

"Sit down, sit down," she urged us, and immediately launched into a long list of complaints: the niggardly service, the terrible food that gave her heartburn, and finally—here she lowered her voice—a conspiracy against her.

"But, dear Henryka, what sort of a conspiracy could that be?"

"Shhhhh . . . ." She put her finger to her lips. "Don't talk so loud." She looked around furtively, then with startling strength pulled me by the arm, closer to her. "They understand everything here," she said.

"They understand Polish?" I whispered back. Henryka nodded, puffing out her lower lip conspiratorially. She sat on her bed and ordered me to pull up the screen. Only then would she explain the mysterious plot.

"Those who do this"—here she raised her hand—"are against me. Just look around, you will notice it immediately. And those who do this"—she put her palms together, as if in prayer, and bent forward in an Oriental bow—"are with me. But we shall fight back, we shall act all together . . . only patience . . . be patient . . . be calm . . . one must be calm and wait . . . patiently . . . ."

|||

It was an early autumn afternoon, one of those last hot days when the torrid air hangs heavily over the earth. The funeral home, a small, white, one-story building with a row of cinnamon chrysanthemums fading in the heat along one side, seemed strangely out of place in the midst of the encroaching city. High-rise buildings pressed in from all sides, and it was obvious that in a few months, a few short years at the most, the building and its small chapels would disappear under the blade of a bulldozer.

The funeral procession was soon formed: in front, a long black hearse with Henryka de Chatin's casket, followed by a shabby Chevrolet belonging to the priest and an MG driven by a thin, freckled young man with flaxen hair who had been talking to the priest earlier. The driver of the lead car got behind the wheel briskly and signaled that he was about to leave. Everyone drove slowly at first, stopping at the lights, but as soon as they reached the beltway the lead car sped up to sixty miles an hour and the others followed suit, until they turned off onto a side road that shortly became a narrow country road dotted with potholes. The road went up and down over the hills, winding this way and that until it sank in a ravine. A sudden calm fell over the cortege, a slightly disquieting silence under a gray cloud of dust rising from under the car wheels. As they drove up a steep hill, the dusty cloud settled down, and an open, bright landscape came into view, bathed in sunshine. Open fields ran along both sides, the corn still green and its plumes standing high. A vast blue sky lined with woolly white clouds seemed almost to touch the earth.

The road still climbed steeply, ever closer to heaven. At the top of the hill, the road plunged down amid fields of ripe orange pumpkins, but the hearse stopped on the crest, high above the scattered prosperous farms with their white homesteads.

It was the kind of view yearned for by those who live within the four walls of lonely rooms, those who suffocate in subways on hot afternoons, those who are sick, those who are sad, those who are dying.

Suddenly, as if out of nowhere, there rose before them, lost in this generous abundance of earth, sky, and sun, a small, flat cemetery surrounded by an iron fence. It was a small plot, with flat headstones planted firmly in the ground, the grass still green between rows, and only here and there an orange-gold maple leaf fluttering gently in the soft, warm breeze.

The mourners stood aside, letting the young man go first. He kept turning back. It was obvious he was embarrassed by the whole ritual. But it did not take long. The priest spoke a few romantic words about invisible threads binding us together forever. Then he took off his stole and walked back with the youth. An elderly couple joined them, Henryka's Quaker friends who had allowed her to be buried in their cemetery plot.

"Your father could not come to the funeral?" the elderly woman asked gently. The youth shook his head.

"Does he know?"

"Not yet. I'm going to see him soon, and then I'll tell him. I will go tomorrow."

"Is it true your father is feeling a little better?"

"So it seems," said the boy. He had never visited his father at the hospital, but now he decided he would go. It did not matter so much now.

I looked at the boy. He had the strong profile of his grandmother and the same aggressive chin, but his complexion was light, and his forehead and the sides of his nose were covered with tiny freckles. He was tall and slim and looked no more than twenty-two.

We stood in the yard at the entrance to the cemetery, a vast square planted on all sides with old maple trees. At the highest point, close to the road, there was a podium of sorts, a few stone steps ending abruptly in the air.

"What is that?" I asked.

"A pulpit. The steps seem to lead straight to heaven, don't they?"

"Or the stage setting for a Greek tragedy," I thought. For on those steps, a chorus of elders could stand and close the priest's sermon with the final words of the tragedy of Jocasta:

> Therefore beware, O mortal creature,
> And watch the signs of coming days:
> The battle of our lives has not been won
> Until the tale is all unraveled,
> Until the darkness falls
> And pain has ceased.*

Translated by Nina Dyke

---

*Sophocles, *Oedipus Rex.*

Found in Translation

A New Chapter in American Literature

THE PUBLICATION IN ENGLISH of these two novellas by Danuta Mostwin opens a new chapter in the history of the literature of the United States and in the appreciation of Polish-American literature. For far too long, many academicians restricted the canon of American literature to the writings of the Brahmins of the Northeast. Eventually, as the country grew, they expanded the canon to include the literary efforts of similar classes in other parts of the country. In time, they recognized literature from other segments of society but often only under the designation of local color. By the early twentieth century, developments like the Harlem Renaissance had brought the literature of African Americans to the attention of the literary public;[1] eventually, albeit rather slowly, African-American literature was admitted to the canon. In a similar manner, by midcentury, it had become impossible to ignore the literary productivity and quality of Jewish-American authors; the canon began to recognize and feature the significant contributions of Jewish writers.[2] Under the impetus of this extension of the canon and in conjunction with social developments in the country, the literature penned by immigrants to the United States and by their children began to receive attention— although that attention was slow to take hold, was restricted to works written in English, and generally was granted only to selected immigrant groups. By the late 1960s, Hispanic and Native American authors had begun to command long-overdue attention, and today they are not only recognized but regularly included in most classes on American literature.[3] These expansions of the canon have brought long-overlooked writers and works of quality literature to the attention of readers in the United States, and they more honestly and accurately mirror the global makeup of American society.

More recently, another past-due and exciting development has occurred: more and more attention is being directed toward literature, both past and contemporary, written in languages other than English by residents of the United States—many of them immigrants, but some of them the children of immigrants—and even by visitors to this country. Among the scholars who have championed this movement is Werner Sollors, whose works have defended the proposition that American literature is historically and properly multilingual, supported the recovery of important foreign-language texts, and promoted an openness to current authors writing in languages other than English.[4] This most recent expansion of the canon requires study and appreciation of these literary works in the languages in which they are written; but it also demands quality translations of the works if the general public is to recognize and profit from the experiences and insights of these authors and their ethnic or racial groups.

These admissions to the canon, especially in the realm of immigrant literature, have not always been extended to all groups, and among the groups that have received only modest attention are Poles and Polish Americans. The reasons for this are complex; explanations can be found in the failure of the Polish-American community to promote and properly support its writers and in the general indifference, with a few notable exceptions, of the American literary establishment toward this group.

It was once commonly thought that Polish immigrants of the mass immigration—roughly 1880 to 1920—in their rush to survive and adjust to a new country did not produce or even read literature. Such a position is no longer tenable. Recent research has documented a huge body of literature, both prose and poetry, written by and for the burgeoning Polish immigrant community. That very extensive body of literature largely has been ignored, and much of it is being lost because it was written primarily in Polish and published in a myriad of newspapers and journals long since defunct and poorly preserved.[5] Additionally, much of it was of little interest to later waves of immigrants from Poland, whose experiences reflected other realities and concerns. Polish immigrants who arrived after World War II also produced a considerable body of literature; but it, too, was generally written in Polish, a language already commonly discarded by the children of earlier Polish immigrants, and consequently reached only restricted audiences. Other figures, such as Czesław Miłosz, who fled Poland during the Cold War, frequently commanded not only national but international attention and recognition. But they generally addressed only Polish topics in their writings and never thought of themselves as American writers. Finally, in the past quarter-century, further waves of immigrants have arrived from Poland (e.g., Solidarity refugees from martial law in the 1980s, and now immigrants from free Poland). These latest groups have also produced writers of note. Perhaps even more than earlier Polish immigrant authors, these writers represent divergent experiences and interests. They write almost exclusively in Polish. Many reside in the United States only temporarily and do not really examine the American scene, while others apparently have taken up permanent residence in this country and write more and more about their American experiences.[6]

This is not to say that there was no Polish-American literature in English until very recently. By the 1930s a number of Polish-American authors were beginning to write in English, and by the 1950s and 1960s English had become the language of preference among American-born authors of Polish descent. None of these writers is likely ever to be regarded as a major literary figure, but there is little doubt that some of them deserve more attention than they have received—if one is to judge by the minor authors of other ethnic and immigrant communities. Literature in English, however, did not become common in the Polish-American community until after World War II.[7] Only today are Polish-American writers such as Anthony Bukoski, Suzanne Strempek Shea, Leslie Pietrzyk, Gary Gildner, Stuart Dybek, Anne Pellowski, Margaret Szumowski, and Jan Guzlowski telling the Polish-American story in English and beginning to command national and even international audiences.[8]

Still, in general, Polish-American literature is much neglected, and there can be no doubt that one major reason for this neglect is that so much of the Polish-American community's literature has been written in Polish. This is one reason—but only one reason—why the current translation is so important and welcome. It is, one hopes, only the first of many such translations that will make available to general audiences a more accurate record and appreciation of Polish-American literature—a literature rich in diversity of experience and expression.

The novellas here translated deal with what is perhaps the most neglected chapter of the Polish-American experience. The stories of Polish displaced persons and political refugees who fled to the United States in the aftermath of World War II and during the Cold War are, in all likelihood, the least publicized segments of Polish-American history. Almost all who told these stories did so in Polish and, consequently, they had little or no access to general American audiences. They also had only limited audiences in the Polish-American community itself because, as noted above, the children and grandchildren of the immigrants of the late nineteenth and early twentieth centuries were themselves less than fluent in Polish. Additionally, they frequently told a story that the United States had no desire to hear because it treated the abandonment of the longest-fighting member of the Allied nations to Soviet hegemony. To complicate matters even more, these authors had no qualms about informing people in the West of the failures of communism at a time when a good many Western intellectuals, politicians, media pundits, and literary figures were sympathetic to the Soviet experiment.

Danuta Mostwin is herself a post–World War II Polish immigrant to the Unites States. Not only has she lived the experiences of that generation of Polish immigrants but she has studied, researched, and taught them, as well. She is a scholar, a teacher, and a writer. There are few others as well qualified to tell this chapter of the Polish-American story.

Finally, there are the stories here selected: *Jocasta* and *The Last Will of Blaise Twardowski.* These novellas reflect important aspects of the generations of immigrants with which they deal. Furthermore, many of the topics that they address are the very ones frequently overlooked in the writings of other immigrant groups and of other generations of Polish immigrants; consequently, the topics are little considered by the reading public. Perhaps most important, these works are significant not only for the insights they share and the reminders they provide but also for the questions they raise about the experiences treated and about the features of those experiences that are left unaddressed. Like all good literature, these stories challenge readers to go beyond the narrative at hand. For all these reasons, the current volume is a valuable resource for readers in general and for teachers of the immigrant experience, ethnic and Polish studies, feminist literature, and American literature and culture.

This is not the place for a detailed analysis of literary techniques employed in the two novellas, but brief note must be taken of the skill with which these stories are crafted. One strong feature of both novellas, perhaps the central feature of each, is characterization; indeed, it is the main characters of these stories who carry the burden of conveying the major themes of the works. Henryka de Chatin (formerly Henryka Szatkowska), Błażej Twardowski, and Jan Wieniawski are complex, three-dimensional figures intelligently and skillfully drawn. The reader comes to know them through a variety of means, including the opinions of other characters and direct observation of their behavior, speech, and thoughts. Most important, the success of their characterization allows readers to come to terms with the issues with which Mostwin is dealing. In passing, one might also add that even the minor characters in these stories are well-drawn, complex, and fascinating. Greta and Jan de Chatin, for example, although not protagonists in *Jocasta*, play significant roles in that story, and the same can be said of Stefański and Dekrocki in *The Last Will of Blaise Twardowski*.

Contributing to this successful characterization—and also well handled in its own right—is the author's use of point of view. Mostwin's choice of a first-person, limited point of view in *Jocasta* engages readers with the complexities of Henryka de Chatin's personality, allowing them to come to their own conclusions about her character while providing them with the insights of a (seemingly) reliable narrator. In a different vein, Mostwin's omniscient narrator of *The Last Will of Blaise Twardowski* gives readers access to the thoughts and opinions of multiple characters who convey the complex issues in this piece.

The action and plot of the novellas are also very deftly handled. In each case, Mostwin violates chronology to achieve her ends. *Jocasta* begins with the narrator's dream about the already dead Henryka de Chatin, and *The Last Will of Blaise Twardowski* opens with Błażej on his deathbed. The main body of each narrative consists of flashbacks in which the reader discovers how events have brought the main characters to the circumstances in which the stories begin. This strategy relieves readers of the burden of suspense (they already know that Henryka is dead and that Błażej is dying and struggling with decisions about his estate) and focuses their attention on how and why things have turned out as they have. In effect, Mostwin's approach accentuates her themes and forces her readers to be more reflective.

As these brief comments suggest, *Jocasta* and *The Last Will of Blaise Twardowski* are skillfully wrought narratives; but their place in American literature is merited as much by the topics they address and the insights they provide as by the author's literary talent.

At one level, the themes of these novellas are very common in contemporary American literature. Both pieces, for example, address the pain of old age (especially old age faced in isolation), a gnawing sense of uprootedness, the excruciating complexities of family relations in America, and death; but each novella treats these topics somewhat differently. Both Henryka de Chatin and Błażej Twardowski are old and alone, but their circumstances differ markedly. Henryka comes to America as an aging mother yearning to be reunited with her son and his family. Błażej Twardowski, on the other hand, came to America as young man, has been in this country for fifty years at the time of his story, and has no close family at all in the United States or Poland. In *Jocasta*, the relationships that Mostwin addresses are those of the nuclear family: mother to son, mother-in-law to daughter-in-law, grandmother to grandson, and father to son. *The Last Will of Blaise Twardowski* also considers relationships, but they are primarily the bonds of the extended family and of friendships that fill the void left by an absence of the nuclear family. In both cases, these relationships are complicated by the uprooted lives of the two protagonists. As is the case with so many figures in recent American literature, Henryka de Chatin and Błażej Twardowski suffer from a loss of identity: they are uncertain who they are and where they belong. Finally, both main characters die alone and with no clear resolution of their dilemmas.

For all their similarities, there are also thematic differences between the stories. The distinctions exist at many levels, but the two most obvious are also the most important. As the title of the first novella suggests, *Jocasta* is, in the classic sense, a tragedy, and much of its appeal arises from the fascination that tragedy has always held for audiences. For its part, *The Last Will of Blaise Twardowski* takes up an equally timeless topic: the question of materialism and the proper use of wealth.

Such themes are clearly universal. What makes Mostwin's treatment special is her placement of the themes in the context of the immigrant experience. Furthermore, the immigrant experience is quite specific. It is the Polish-American immigrant experience, and it is the experience of specific generations: in the case of *Jocasta* the post–World War II experience, and in *The Last Will of Blaise Twardowski* the experience of an immigrant of an earlier generation intimately associating with Polish immigrants of the Cold War era. These contexts give special focus to the themes that these novellas explore as a part of American literature.

As a tale of aging and domestic tragedy, *Jocasta* tells a moving and universal story but not a generic one. Every aspect of this novella is grounded in particular circumstances that make it unique. The background of immigration to the United States, the post–World War II era, and the Polish experience all complicate the tale considerably and make *Jocasta* a story new to most American readers.

Henryka and her son Jan undergo a trauma common to most immigrants, but one that generally is not appreciated by the average American—and often not even by the children and grandchildren of these immigrants—one that, until recently, has not been noted adequately in the canon of American literature. This trauma is perhaps best understood as a form of schizophrenia, which, in the case of Henryka, is described in the bond that she shares with the narrator:

> The bond between us, I think, was that we all lived simultaneously in two worlds, not one, and that this split us irrevocably in half. No one who was not "one of us" could ever know us fully, because only one-half of our very selves ever showed—the other was kept in shadow. This cleft, with no sharp edge and indeed sometimes hardly noticeable, was the real danger point. There our madness crouched, ready to pounce at an opportune moment.
>
> No one was really aware of this until, after some years away from the homeland, he had become, in part at least, a different person. It takes time to become acquainted with one's own duality. Sometimes it was possible to ignore it, to hide it, or even to triumph over it, but occasionally a searing flare-up of madness would sweep away all reason. (80)

This "madness" is the key to a proper appreciation of the story, and it extends, in one form or another, to other characters.

The other major victim of this condition is Jan, Henryka's son. For Jan, this sense of duality takes the form of a desire to go home. Indeed, after his accident, Jan is obsessed with a desire to go home, an obsession clearly revealed in a conversation between Jan and Henryka in Pine Grove, the asylum in which Jan is being treated:

> "I want to go home!" he sobbed, "Home!"
>
> "My dearest," she began. She hugged his rigid shoulders and stroked his cheek, covered with gray stubble. "You have no home, you don't have a

home any more. But you must get well. You must make an effort . . . with all your will . . . ."

He looked at her uncomprehendingly. Impatiently he pushed away her hands.

"Home," he repeated. "I want to go home . . . ."

"My boy, my dearest boy, my little Jan." She stroked his motionless hands. "There is no home. Please, you must understand. There is no home left." (96–97)

Two ambiguities make this exchange particularly important. One is uncertainty about the home to which Jan is referring. Is it the home he shares with his wife and son, the home he knew before the war, or simply an expression of his desire to leave the asylum? However one understands this ambiguity, there can be no doubt that Jan's immigrant status, first in Germany and then in the United States, has been a contributing factor in his tragic circumstances. The other ambiguity is the degree to which Henryka bears responsibility for Jan's crisis of homelessness, a consideration that enhances the tragedy of the story and demands consideration, if not resolution, from the reader.

In a minor way, this same duality also affects Jan's wife, Greta, and their son, Henry. This is most clearly communicated in the fact that Greta and Henry "speak only German together" (90). This use of German confirms Greta's native identity but clashes in some measure with her new life in the United States and with her son's identity as an American; and it certainly complicates the relation of Greta and Henry with Jan.

Jocasta is not, however, simply a story of tragedy complicated by the immigrant experience. The characters are immigrants who have lived through the greatest armed conflict in the history of the world, and this deepens the tragedy and the complexity of their lives. The story does not go into great detail on the characters' experiences during the war, but the general outlines of their personal histories are made clear. This approach is undoubtedly correct for the story: *Jocasta* is, after all, not a tale of war but a domestic tragedy set in the United States a decade after the war. Still, the war experiences of the characters give the story a depth and complexity that set it apart from other such works in the American canon.

The story of the Szatkowski family during World War II is sparingly reported; but it is the experience of literally millions of other Poles, and an awareness of it is essential if one is to appreciate fully the achievement of the novella. Henryka's discovery, shortly after her arrival in the United States, of her son, daughter-in-law, and grandson all speaking German creates a crisis that reveals her family's history during the war:

> She ran upstairs quickly, threw herself on the bed, and burst into uncontrollable sobs, stifling her moans in the pillow. Long-forgotten memories now assailed her from all sides. All of 1939 came back to her: the expulsion from their apartment in Poznań; the German order to move east; the provisional evacuation camp out in the open, surrounded by barbed wire; their journey to Warsaw in overcrowded trains; the long lines for permits of all sorts; the lack of accommodations (they'd had no place of their own for a long time); her husband's illness; her husband's death; the Warsaw Uprising; flight from a burning, collapsing house; her daughter's death under the rubble. And all the time, the never-ceasing, deep, painful fear. The sound track of these images moving swiftly in her brain was always the same: it was in German, the same language her son, her daughter-in-law, and her grandson were using at this moment down in the kitchen. (81)

Jan's experiences in a German prisoner-of-war camp illustrate another side of the Polish experience of the war, that of Poles in concentration camps and slave labor camps who became displaced persons after their liberation.

Mostwin does not, however, use her novella to settle scores. Her description of Greta's family during the war provides a counterbalance to Henryka's story and its tragic conclusion:

> Greta was the daughter of a German industrialist, one of those who had passively resisted the Hitler regime and had been tolerated only because of their technical skills. She had grown up in the shadow of fear, in terror of imminent arrest and deportation to a concentration camp. The last months, the last weeks, of the war were the worst. She had lived through the bombings of Berlin and had escaped from their flaming house by jumping from a window. For a long time afterward, she had nightmares. During one long period of depression, she did not leave the house at all but sat in an armchair days on end, holding in her hands a book she could not even read. (74)

Making the tragedy even deeper and more difficult to comprehend, Mostwin describes how Jan acknowledged "how much he owed to Greta and often recalled it in his letters to his mother" (74). Nonetheless, the difficulty of the situation and the poignancy of the tragic relationships are anticipated even before Henryka's arrival by Jan's feelings of guilt about his marriage to Greta:

> Sometimes, however, he was disturbed by a vague feeling of guilt and an ill-defined fear that he had broken some taboo, that he had crossed a line beyond which the path was not so certain and had to be trodden extremely cautiously. This sense of unease assailed him every time he thought about his mother, or his sister, who had died during the bombing of Warsaw, or his father, who had died during the German wartime occupation of Poland. (75)

In addition to the other questions regarding the immigrant experience that *Jocasta* raises, the tragic elements of the story demand analysis. Who bears the blame for the misery that results? Henryka? Jan? Greta? The answer is not easy. Everyone seems flawed. Henryka's scheming and Jan's weakness are obvious; but Greta and even Henry seem to bear some responsibility. Greta, for example, rather insensitively refuses Henryka's invitation to call her "mother" and will not allow Henryka to teach Henry Polish. For his part, Henry seems quite content to be estranged from his father. Like all tragedies, *Jocasta* challenges audiences to understand the forces that govern human existence, to search for tragic flaws in the characters, and to place themselves in the position of the tragic hero. It is the peculiar strength of *Jocasta* that it expands and further complicates the limits of tragedy in American literature.

One other particularly insightful aspect of *Jocasta* demands comment. American literature rarely appreciates the power of language, especially that of an immigrant's native language; and where it does address the issue, it focuses on the tension between the immigrant's native language and English. Mostwin not only understands the power of language in the lives of immigrants but extends exploration of the issue to a wider and more complex linguistic domain. Henryka's "sound track" of the images of her family's experiences in the war is always in German; it is her son's use of that language with his wife and children that, one could argue, sets in motion the events that lead to catastrophe. The issue of language also affects Greta, who becomes "furious" when Henryka begins to teach Henry Polish; she insists that "the boy's mind will be ruined, a third language will confuse him, it is too early,

English and German are quite enough" (83). Eventually, language takes control of Jan's relationship with his family. He feels alienated from his son because the son "spends all his time with his mother"; and he laments that "They speak only German together, and I . . . I am . . . ."(90). On the other hand, one of the bonds that tie him to his mother is Polish: "Though Jan found it hard to admit, he could relax best with his mother. With her, he could speak openly and in Polish, which, in itself, reduced the tension, like taking off a starched collar after a formal dinner at which one did not feel at ease" (88). Here is a feature of the American immigrant experience that few writers grasp and even fewer writers have addressed as seriously and thoughtfully as Mostwin does in *Jocasta.*

The Last Will of Blaise Twardowski is at once simpler and more ambitious than *Jocasta.* Again, Mostwin takes up themes common to American literature and of universal appeal: aging and loneliness. But she deals with those themes in the context of Polish immigrant life, and this adds dimension to the novella. At one level, *The Last Will of Blaise Twardowski* is the moving story of a lonely old man, not always particularly sympathetic, who faces illness and death without the support of family or friends and upon whom distant relatives prey. The immigrant setting of this story, however, is so prominent that one might as easily contend that the story is a study of the community and only secondarily the tale of one member of that community.

However one approaches this novella, two characters clearly dominate: Błażej Twardowski and Jan Wieniawski. And Mostwin clearly wants her audience to compare and contrast these two inhabitants of Broad Street and to reflect on their relationship. To all appearances, Błażej is the protagonist of the piece; in many—but not all—respects, he is a representative of the period of mass immigration during the latter part of the nineteenth century and the early part of the twentieth century. He emigrated from Poland "for bread," worked for almost fifty years in a steel mill in the United States, and managed to acquire a small fortune. He also displays the trauma common to immigrant life: a confusion of identity resulting from his loss of connection to the old world and from his failure to establish comparable personal relations in his new world. Indeed, Błażej eventually surrenders even his memories of Jan Lipa, his closest friend in Poland, who became a priest and was killed by the Russians during World War II and who, in many ways, symbolizes what

Błażej has left behind. Early in the story, Mostwin summarizes the circumstances that govern Błażej's life:

> He forgot about Jasiek and about the village and its affairs, too. He was no
> longer "Błażek" [his nickname in Poland] but "Mister Blaise Twardowski."
> There was no room in his new life for the village or Jasiek Lipa—or even a
> memory of them—or any remembrance of that gratitude of long ago or of
> that feeling of trust, once coaxed into life and now buried forever in the
> ashes of an abandoned fire.
>
> "What did anyone ever give me there?" Błażej would say. "An empty
> belly, that's what. There was nothing to eat there. You couldn't buy a pair
> of shoes."
>
> There was only Błażej Twardowski, the steelworks, and Broad Street.
> (15)

Błażej never manages to compensate for these losses, even though he has
amassed a significant estate.

Ultimately, "old and sick and lonely," Błażej yearns for the world he
left behind and for Jasiek:

> And now . . . lonely, he cried for that long-past day, for that generosity,
> and, perhaps, out of longing for the Błażej of long ago. For that one had
> been a boy of fire and hope, resolute and unyielding.
>
> "You are so smart, Błażek," Jasiek Lipa had marveled. "You should go
> to school. You'll go far."
>
> "Who knows?" Błażek had answered, "Maybe I will."
>
> "You know what?" Jasiek had said, "If you have a son, make him study
> to be a priest or a teacher. Spare no money. I'll help him. I'll teach him and
> guide him," he promised. "He'll be a priest or a doctor or an engineer. He'll
> be an educated man. But it takes money."
>
> Now that he was old and sick and lonely, Twardowski missed the young
> Błażek and the tart taste of hard pears. He had money, it was true, but he
> had no son. (41–42)

Precisely these memories and regrets lead Błażej to place one condition on
the estate that he decides to leave to distant relatives in Poland, although they
had attempted to take advantage of him in the past: "They must send their
children to schools, not drive them to work too early, but educate them to be
priests or doctors or teachers. That's my condition" (65–66). The story ends,

however, on a note of irony and ambiguity because Błażej's "last will" is certain to be challenged by a distant American cousin who was the beneficiary of his previous will but who had refused to use the money to educate her son.

Thus, one part of the novella features the personal story of Błażej; but Mostwin extends that story to other members of Błażej's immediate circle of acquaintances and, thus, broadens the reader's perspective. The other major figure in this story is Jan Wieniawski: the owner of a travel office, Błażej's confidant, and, in the final analysis, his only real friend in America. Jan plays such a significant role in the novella that one could argue that the story is as much his as Błażej's. Minimally, he is a foil to Błażej and allows the reader to see another generation of the Polish immigrant experience and the ways in which various generations interact. Although the men share the common denominator of the immigrant experience, their different temperaments, backgrounds, and perceptions set apart Błażej and Jan—and set apart one wave of Polish immigrants from another:

> Both men had been washed up onto Broad Street by the waves of the bay. Błażej had accepted this philosophically, matter-of-factly, and had adapted himself and even grown fond of his new surroundings. But in Wieniawski there seethed an unending rebellion and bitterness. What would have become of him, though, were it not for Broad Street and his newly opened travel office, the Albatross? (18)

The different responses of the two men, however, seem dictated by more than disposition; the circumstances of their immigration also are stressed:

> Anyway, Wieniawski was a grumbler. He would have grumbled no matter where in the world he found himself, except, perhaps, in the old country or among understanding friends. But here he was alone, damn it, completely alone. He grumbled more to bemoan his own loneliness than anything else, and Broad Street just happened to be there to provide a handy target for his abuse. He thought it squalid, noisy, stinking, and tawdry. He deplored having to live in such degradation amid uncomprehending strangers. Wieniawski's life had begun and developed in the old country. Unlike Błażej, he talked about the old country with genuine emotion, never failing to add that it was the West and its politics that were to blame for his own forced migration to the United States. He always stressed the fact that he was a political émigré, crushed by an evil whim of fate and forced to vegetate on Broad Street, of no use to either the old country or the new. (17–18)

Finally, Mostwin accurately describes the tensions that arise among the different generations of immigrants. Wieniawski, although himself of peasant stock, cannot relate to earlier peasant immigrants:

> "And those people . . . ," he sighed, thinking of the "bread immigrants" who clustered along Broad Street. "Those people . . . God have mercy! Mistrustful, suspicious, hostile. Back in Poland, I knew the peasants. Knew the workers, too. They were my people. I could always talk with them. But here . . . They are so changed in America, it is as if they have come from another planet." (18)

Here is material that not only complicates the story of Błażej's loneliness and "last will"; it is a separate story, one virtually unexplored in American literature.

Two other figures play a role in Błażej's declining years: Stefański, the Polish-born organist for a local church and a worker at Jan Wieniawski's travel office, and Antek Dekrocki, a Polish-American lawyer also working with Wieniawski. Stefański is a recent immigrant who, in Błażej's opinion, talks "different" and who has no use for Błażej. The gulf that separates Błażej and Stefański is even wider than the one that divides Wieniawski and Błażej; for Stefański represents a third generation of Polish immigrants: "The truth was that Stefański—the Party's prize pupil, the pride of the People's Republic, the flower of the new communist elite, the respected and admired official—had chosen freedom" (22). In his own way, Stefański serves as a foil to both Błażej and Wieniawski. Błażej's naive question "[I]t's better over here?" (22) goads Stefański simply to retort, "If only I could, I'd go back. I'd just as soon leave the United States. What sort of life can one have here? . . ." (22). He is also very different from Wieniawski, even though he, like Wieniawski, is a political émigré. Unlike Wieniawski, he has no particular love for Poland. When he discovers that Błażej's Polish relatives have been taking advantage of the old man, his response is broad and sweeping: "Let me tell you—they're all bastards, every one of them." To make his point even more emphatically, he adds, "Let me tell you—they're not worth a damn! I know them. For a dollar, they'd hack one another to pieces. Well, let them. Good riddance!" (37). When reprimanded by Wieniawski, Stefański attempts to clarify: "I'm talking about the communists. What's with you? Are you on their side?" (37). This does not, however, placate Wieniawski:

"I won't spit on my own people. I wasn't raised by the communists. I got nothing from them. You got everything. Let me tell you something, Mr. Stefański: you are an unhappy man. I feel sorry for you. I feel more sorry for you than for those people over there or for those here, for that matter." (37)

The Polish-American community, it would appear, is much more diverse than one might have supposed.

Rounding out Mostwin's portrait of that community is Antek Dekrocki, a lawyer and Wieniawski's partner. Dekrocki represents the American-born members of the Polish-American community. His minor, but not insignificant, role indicates quite clearly that Mostwin's primary focus is on the immigrant segment of the community, not on what one today might call its ethnic component. Nonetheless, Dekrocki's identity is deliberately and clearly established:

Dekrocki was born here and raised here, and it was from here that he took off, as from a springboard, up and away from the immigrant ethnic group he came from. His parents had given him a good education and passed on to him a vague feeling of love for the misty old country.

During his army days, he had met some Poles who immediately had wanted to make him over after their own fashion. They had become his friends, but failed to change him in any way. His respect for his parents and his friendship for his old army buddies brought him closer to Wieniawski and helped him bear with equanimity his partner's tart tongue and his endless Polish tirades. (45–46)

Here, then, is another generation in the story—and another perspective on the immigrant experience and the immigrant community. In terms of this story, at least, one might surmise that in Mostwin's opinion the children and the grandchildren of Polish immigrants occupy interesting ground; they have neither lost their ethnic identity as quickly as some had predicted nor retained it as well as others might have hoped.

Thus, although the primary focus of the story is on the immigrants and their experience, Mostwin insists on a recognition of the community's complexity. At a crucial point in the novella, the first time Błażej sends money off to his relatives Poland, all four major figures participate:

Błażej was counting out the money stolidly, handing it over to Dekrocki. Stefański looked on with interest. The four of them, all with last names ending in "ski," were now gathered in the front room of the office. Twardowski, the eldest of them, had come to America half a century before. Dekrocki had been born here. Wieniawski was a political immigrant: he had come after World War II. And Stefański, raised in communist postwar Poland, had chosen freedom. Yet here they were, all together, all Poles. (26)

In precisely this fashion, Mostwin links the two major threads in her novella: the story of Błażej and her portrait of the community.

Jocasta and *The Last Will of Blaise Twardowski* are powerful and provocative novellas, and these brief remarks are intended to promote discussion of the stories, not to close it. Questions naturally arise.

Those questions generally may be sorted into two categories: those concerning what the stories say and those concerning what they leave unsaid. In both cases, however, the questions generally reflect comparisons and contrasts between the readers' analyses of the novellas and their experience with and knowledge of the Polish-American immigrant community.

A few examples illustrate the point. In *Jocasta,* for instance, readers may ask whether the tragic relationship between Henryka and Jan is, indeed, the inevitable result of a particular set of personal or historic circumstances. They may speculate whether the experiences of the Szatkowski/de Chatin family during the war justify and explain the behavior of mother and son or, for that matter, whether Greta's attitudes and conduct are explicable in the light of her own experiences. Along these same lines, some readers may challenge the concept that language has power in the lives of the characters in the story. In any case, readers are invited to inquire at every turn whether the behavior of the characters and the course of the plot provide accurate insights into the community in which the story is set.

Perhaps even more questions arise regarding *The Last Will of Blaise Twardowski.* Readers may inquire whether the various generations of the Polish immigrant experience presented by the characters in the story are correctly identified and adequately defined. Furthermore, the conflicts between generations may be taken up by readers whose experiences suggest other relationships. Certainly the description of the Poland and the attitudes of the different characters toward the "old country" will incite different reactions, as will the manner in which the Polish immigrant community in America is described.

A different line of questions arises from the topics that the novellas omit. Certainly no book can be judged solely on the basis of what it doesn't say or address, and no book can be expected to tell the entire story of a community; but it seems likely that many readers will feel that key markers of the Polish immigrant experience (e.g., nativist hostility, discrimination, interracial encounters, and fraternal and sororal organizations) have been overlooked. Discussions and analyses of these markers may be one of the side benefits generated by the novellas; Mostwin deserves credit for encouraging such examinations of the larger Polish immigrant experience.

Finally, these translations force serious questions about the American experience and American literature. They ask whether the canon of American literature is interested enough to consider the Polish experience in the United States and whether it is sophisticated enough to include works translated from Polish. If it is not, American literature will be not only incomplete, it will be poorer.

Thomas J. Napierkowski

Notes

1. Poets, novelists, and playwrights like Langston Hughes, Jean Toomer, Countee Cullen, Claude McKay, Eric Waldron, Zora Neale Hurston, and Arna Bontemps established for African Americans a literary voice that demanded to be heard.

2. In the case of Jewish-American writers, fiction writers such as J. D. Salinger, Norman Mailer, Saul Bellow, Mark Harris, Philip Roth, and Bernard Malamud have commanded the most attention; but poets such as Karl Shapiro and Allen Ginsberg and playwrights, especially Arthur Miller, also made it impossible to ignore the Jewish contribution to American literature.

3. The breakthrough of Hispanic literature was led primarily by Chicano and Chicana authors and by Puerto Rican and *Nuyorican* writers (Puerto Rican authors in New York). The former group includes writers such as Oscar "Zeta" Acosta, Rudolpho Anaya, Raymond Barrio, Nash Candelaria, Tomás Rivera, Richard Vasquez, and José Antonio Villarreal; the latter two groups include authors such as Jesús Colón, Pedro Pietri, Pedro Juan Soto, and Piri Thomas. Native-American novelists like N. Scott Momaday and Leslie Marmon Silko and poets such as Joy Harjo, Simon J. Ortiz, Mary Tall Mountain, and Ray Young Bear, among others, are recognized in the canon.

4. See, for example, *Multilingual America*, edited by Werner Sollors (New York: New York University Press, 1998) and *The Multilingual Anthology of American Literature*, edited by Marc Shell and Werner Sollors (New York: New York University Press, 2000).

5. See Karen Majewski, *Traitors and True Poles: Narrating a Polish-American Identity, 1880–1939* (Athens: Ohio University Press, 2003) for the best history of fiction written by and for Polish immigrants during this period. Additionally, the bibliography of primary sources that accompanies this remarkable piece of scholarship is the best literary record yet compiled of the literary activity of these Poles of the mass immigration. Of the dozens of writers whom she has identified, Dr. Majewski calls special attention to the works of Helena Staś, Czesław Łukaszkiewicz, Stanisław Osada, Melania Nesterowicz, Stefania Laudyn, Julian Czupka, Henryk Nagiel, M. Alfons Chrostowski, Bronisław Wrotnowski, Telesfor Chełchowski, Kazimierz Neuman, Józef Orłowski, and Stanisława Romanowska. For some sense of the equally impressive level of poetic activity during this same period, see Thomas J. Napierkowski, "Three Polish American Poets: Their Significance and Challenge to Polonia," in *Ethnicity. Culture. City*, ed. Thomas Gladsky, Adam Walaszek, and Matgorzata Wawrykiewicz (Warsaw: Oficyna Naukowa, 1998), 325–45. A sample of the poetry is collected in *Antologia Poezji Polsko-Amerykańskiej*, edited by Tadeusz Mitana (Chicago: Polski Klub Artystyczny, 1937).

6. Polish authors writing in the United States during the last fifty or sixty years can be organized into a number of possible time frames or movements that are open to various interpretations. Dr. Anna Jaroszyńska-Kirchmann, surely the leading authority on the subject, has suggested the following breakdown and assignment of major writers. The war years and postwar years produced émigré literature by authors such as Jan Lechoń, Kazimierz Wierzyński, Józef Wittlin, and Aleksander Janta. Following the war and subsequent resettlement of displaced persons and political émigré, Polish authors such as Danuta Mostwin, Alicja Iwańska, Wiesław Kuniczak, and Aleksander Hertz lived and wrote in the United States. During the Cold War, Maria Kuncewicz, Czesław Miłosz, Melchior Wańkowicz, Leopold Tyrmand, and others settled and wrote in this country. Finally, the Solidarity and post-Solidarity years have featured authors such as Stanisław Barańczak, Zofia Mierzejewska, Janusz Głowacki, Kazimierz Braun, Wacław Chabrowski, Anna Frajlich, Henryk Grynberg, Adam Lizakowski, and many others who are difficult to track because they resided only temporarily in the United States. (E-mail to author, October 29, 2003.)

7. Novelists such as Antoni Gronowicz, Wanda Luzenska Kubiak, and Armine von Tempski and short story writers such as Monica Krawczyk, Ed Falkowski, and Peter Mankowski led the way with fiction. In the area of poetry, which still requires a great deal of research and which may have been the literary mode of choice among the immigrants themselves, Edmond Kowalewski, Jan Drechney, Edward Symanski (Symans), Helen Bristol, and Victoria Janda, among others, produced substantial collections. Details on these authors can be found in Joseph Zurawski's *Polish American History and Culture: A Classified Bibliography* (Chicago: Polish Museum of America, 1975).

8. Other Polish-American writers such as Ellen Slezak, Ken Parejko, Jan Minczewski, and Linda Nemec Foster are also attracting growing attention.

The Fiction of Danuta Mostwin

Dom Starej Lady [House of the Old Lady]. London: Veritas, 1958.

Ameryko! Ameryko! [America! America!]. Paris: Instytut Literacki, 1961.

Asteroidy [Asteroids]. London: Polska Fundacja Kulturalna, 1965.

Olivia. Paris: Instytut Literacki, 1965.

Ja za wodą, ty za wodą . . . [Beyond the Waters, You and I]. Paris: Instytut Literacki, 1972.

Odchodzą moji synowie [My Sons Are Leaving]. London: Polska Fundacja Kulturalna, 1977.

Cień księdza Piotra [The Shadow of Father Piotr]. Warsaw: Instytut Wydawniczy "PAX," 1985.

Odkrywanie Ameryki [Discovering America]. Lublin: Norbertinum, 1992.

Tajemnica zwyciężonych [Secret of the Vanquished]. London: Polska Fundacja Kulturalna, 1992.

Nie ma domu [There Is No Home]. Lublin: Norbertinum, 1996.

Słyszę, jak śpiewa Ameryka [I Hear America Singing]. London: Polska Fundacja Kulturalna, 1998.

Szmaragdowa zjawa [The Emerald Specter]. Warsaw: Instytut Wydawniczy "PAX," 1998.

Pisma [Writings], 20 vols. Toruń: Oficyna Wydawnicza Kucharski, 2004–.

9 780821 416082